Blue is the Night

EOIN MCNAMEE

FABER & FABER

First published in 2014
by Faber and Faber Limited
Bloomsbury House
74–77 Great Russell Street
London WC1B 3DA

Typeset by Faber and Faber Ltd
Printed and bound by CPI Group (UK) Ltd, Croydon CR0 4YY

A CIP record for this book
is available from the British Library

ISBN 978–0–571–27860–2

2 4 6 8 10 9 7 5 3 1

12TH NOVEMBER 1952

The Glen, Whiteabbey. Lancelot Curran had bought the Glen shortly after the trial of Robert Taylor for the murder of Mary McGowan in 1949. No record had been kept as to the builder of the house or the year of its construction. It was a large house at the end of a long avenue lined with aspen, pine and birch trees. The avenue led down to the Whiteabbey Road and to the sea. The name of the house had been intended to convey the sense of some Arcadian setting, leafy and gentle. But the glens recalled by the Scottish lowlanders who had settled this coast were not Arcadian. They were places of ambuscade and murder. Genocidal shadows lingered.

The family housekeeper, Mrs McCrink, didn't like being alone in the house after dark, so she finished at four on winter evenings if the Currans were out. It was a rainy evening and it was to be a dark night. Mrs McCrink had closed the front door behind her. Judge Curran had not allowed her a key. Curran was strict about keys. Mrs McCrink knew that the Judge's wife, Doris, had lost hers, and that he had not given her a new one. If the family were out, then Mrs Curran had to climb through a back bedroom window. Mrs McCrink said that it was not dignified for Mrs Curran to climb through windows.

On the way down the drive the wind from the lough tore at the shrubs and trees. It was a black wind and Mrs McCrink drew her coat around her and wished that she had left earlier. Whiteabbey had been a monastic settlement and Mrs McCrink believed that there were hauntings, old stirrings.

On the mid-point angle of the drive McCrink almost cried out when she saw a shape coming towards her. Later she said that she thought she had met a figure of premonition or of judgement coming to her out of the turbulent night. She remembered that Doris played bridge in Whiteabbey on a Thursday afternoon and would return home at that time. Doris was wearing a headscarf and gaberdine raincoat and had her head bent. As she drew level Mrs McCrink spoke her name but Doris did not reply. Mrs McCrink spoke again and Doris looked up this time. Mrs McCrink said afterwards that considering the events of the night to come she wished that Doris had not looked at her. It was like somebody you met in a hospital. It was a hollow-cheeked, asylum look, someone shuffling in a sanatorium corridor.

Mrs McCrink knew that Doris 'had her moments'. She would go into her bedroom and lock the door. Patricia would knock on the door for hours. *Mother, let me in.* But Doris would not answer. Mrs McCrink was aware that there were tensions between nineteen-year-old Patricia and her mother but said that it was 'not her place' to intervene.

Mrs McCrink stood to the side of the avenue and watched Doris walk towards the house until she was lost in the drizzle and the dusk. Afterwards she told people she knew that there was something different about that evening. People were happy to believe her. This is the night when the Curran family begin to recede from the everyday. That their names are appended to the night's roster of bedlamites and fanatics, the damned and the dead. Mrs McCrink walked to the empty gatehouse to the lodge, then turned and looked back. It seemed as if she looked into the darkness of some forest, a storied place, set about with old tellings.

Patricia Curran died later that night. Her body was found on the driveway to the Glen. She had been stabbed thirty-seven times. One year later, twenty-seven-year-old army conscript Iain Hay Gordon was convicted of the murder. His conviction was overturned in 2000. The mystery of Patricia's death has never been solved. Doris Curran was incarcerated in Holywell Mental Hospital and did not leave it until her death. Desmond Curran, Patricia's renegade brother, left the law and turned papish, a Roman Catholic missionary priest. Lance Curran moved to England in 1964, where he remarried following the death of his wife.

One

1ST FEBRUARY 1961

Her name is Doris Agnes Curran. She was born in 1896 in Kent, England. In 1953 she was committed to Holywell mental institution, where she now resides. Her son Desmond is a Roman priest. Her husband Lancelot is a judge and privy councillor. Her daughter Patricia was murdered by a hand unknown in November 1952. Harry Ferguson visits her sometimes. Ferguson used to be her husband's employee in election matters and in many other things. He comes to see her. He sits in front of her in the Holywell mental hospital and pretends that he is interested in her welfare but she knows what really interests him and that is her dead daughter Patricia.

'How long is it since Patricia died?'

'Nine years.'

'I wonder what happened to her Juliet cap?' Doris said. Patricia's hair was not like her mother's, long and silky. Patricia's was dark and wiry. She kept it from her face with two clips to either side and she wore a yellow Juliet cap to keep it in place.

'The Juliet cap was found the morning after,' Ferguson said, 'by the drive. As if someone had left it there, for nobody found it that night.'

'A Juliet cap sits at the crown of your head, and can be adorned with pearls, beading, or any other materials that co-ordinate with your gown. You can wear a Juliet cap alone, or use it to attach a veil. The Juliet cap style is not something we regularly see, but it's undeniably pretty and unusual.'

'You have a great memory for some things, Mrs Curran.'

And not for others. Doris remembers seeing the cap flung on the chair in the hallway. Patricia was always careless with her things and slapdash in her manner.

'Has Desmond written to you?'

Her son Desmond went to Africa. With the Bible in his hand, bringing the word to the natives like Livingstone. There was a globe of the Earth in the hallway and he would hold it between his hands and say is this all of it, Mother, is this all the world? Desmond was a solemn boy, Wednesday's child full of woe. Patricia wasn't like that. Her eyes would follow Doris wherever she went. She would find herself checking her hair or if her slip was showing. Doris said to Lance that she was on parade every day in her own house like a guardsman on Horse Guards'. Lance replied that Patricia was only a child. The two of them were always thick as thieves.

There was something about Patricia that she could not understand. Even as a baby she was independent. Doris had dreamed of having a daughter. She turned the word motherhood over in her head. But when Patricia looked at her she kept seeing the pale, medicated stare of the murderesses in Broadmoor.

'Do you remember the first time I came to your house, Mrs Curran?'

'The Glen.'

'No, your first house. On the Malone Road. After the Taylor murder.'

'The knave.'

'Sorry.'

'I thought of him as a character from a card game.'

'I see.'

Doris had attended Cheltenham Ladies' College. They did tarot readings in the dormitory at night. There are other worlds. The names of the cards frightened her. The empress. The hanged man. Judgement. The ouija board frightened her, she didn't have to be told there were other worlds. And one night they sat around a table holding hands in a séance, five girls in nightdresses with the lights out. You waited for candles flickering in eerie draughts, eyes rolling back in the head. She waited for the silence to be broken. She waited for a voice to say *I am Thomas Cutbush*.

'Maybe you don't recall.'

'I recall it perfectly.'

Lance was not home in the evening, which was commonplace. Desmond was doing his modelling. Patricia had taken the bridge cards from the card-table drawer and was playing patience with them on the floor. Patricia knew she was not allowed to handle the expensive Waddington cards but Doris quenched her irritation. The family rarely spent time together in this manner and Doris was determined not to start an argument.

At such times Doris thought they could be a real family, a true family of evening walks and civility over the dinner table, but they lived in a house of silences, varied so that Doris thought you could write them down in a book like a catalogue of all the silences there ever were.

Desmond had answered the door to Ferguson.

'Is the Attorney General home?'

'Father isn't here. Is everything all right?'

'Nothing that affects the family, Desmond, but a woman has been slain in Newington.'

'I see. Come in, Mr Ferguson.'

Curran had bought a house on the Malone Road in Belfast in 1947. Doris wanted to be close to the city and the picture houses, although the city was nothing like London and there was nothing of the glamour of Piccadilly or walks in Hyde Park or Regent's Park with nursemaids pushing carriages.

Doris came to the doorway of the drawing room as Ferguson entered the hall.

'Good evening, Mr Ferguson. Desmond, bring Mr Ferguson

in to the fire. There is a strange chill to the night air, isn't there? I think it's because the city is built on a swamp.'

'Mother doesn't like living in the provinces,' Patricia said. 'She doesn't see why we have to live out here in the benighted sticks. Can a stick be benighted?'

'Stop moaning, Patricia,' Desmond said. 'Mr Ferguson doesn't want to listen to your spoiled meanderings. Someone has been murdered.'

'A murder?' Patricia was kneeling on the floor in front of the fire. Looking up into Ferguson's face. Alert and troubled.

'A lady killed in her own home.'

'Mr Curran will want to be told,' Doris said. 'He may be at the Reform Club.'

'I looked in the club but he hadn't been in.'

Desmond turned his back on Ferguson. He sat down at a card table placed against the wall. There were half-finished models of warships on the table. The Tirpitz. The Graf Spee. There were balsa shavings on the floor. There were miniature tins of Humbrol for painting the models. Desmond had built a Spitfire which hung from his bedroom ceiling on fishing line. The table smelt of epoxies and resins. There was a row of sheathed modelling knives. Desmond sitting at the table for hours, his fringe falling over his forehead.

'How is Mrs Ferguson?' Doris said.

'She's fine,' Ferguson said. Doris looking at Ferguson like butter wouldn't melt, Patricia told her friend Hilary Douglas later, though she knows that Esther Ferguson is high-strung as piano wire and a lush to boot. Doris is craftier than anyone thinks, Patricia said, though not all the time.

'I saw her in town the other day,' Patricia said. 'She looked lovely.' Though Patricia told Hilary that Esther's lipstick had been awry and her eyes were glittery.

'It's pleasant to hear you give a compliment, Patricia,' Doris said. 'You so seldom compliment those around you.'

Patricia bowed her head. She had heard the tone in her mother's voice. Before Ferguson had entered the evening had been building around Doris's mood. Desmond and Patricia knew what direction it was taking. There would be slammed doors. There would be long silences. Doris working down through the increments of blame until she reached the rich trove of marital loss, the treasured disappointments. The wasted life. The absent husband. The ungrateful children. This was the wife-bounty. Plundered from the ruins.

'You look lovely too, Mother,' Patricia said in a small voice.

'Your mother is a beautiful dancer,' Ferguson said. He could feel what was going on. The air in the room charged with Doris's mood, the soul-chagrin, and they deferred to it.

'Mother taught me to dance,' Desmond said. 'The Charleston, isn't that right?'

'It was your father taught me,' Doris said. 'The first time I saw it we were at the pictures. Their Own Desire with Norma Shearer. I thought I'd never learn it. I was all elbows and feet.'

'I find that hard to believe,' Ferguson said.

'If Lance were here he could tell you. But he is not.'

He saw Desmond and Patricia exchange a look. He glanced at his watch. Patricia touched his arm. Now was not the time to go. He knew he should not leave them to it, the familial web of half-truths.

Patricia was wearing a blue satinette dressing gown. She leaned forward to dry her hair before the fire. Ferguson could see the nape of her neck, the poise of her body under the material, the folds and pleatings, the way she gathered the skirt under her, the way it let in glimpses, the word bare and the word skin. She held her hair bunched in one hand and glanced at him from under it, making a funny face that none of the others could see, knowing that he could see her shoulder where the robe had slipped, winking at him with her tongue in the corner of her mouth, bringing a low-key sexual drollery to the moment before dropping her hair over her face again.

'Perhaps Father got lost in the woods,' Patricia said.

Patricia called the garden the woods. No one ever went into the woods. They were like the forest from a tale. There would be clearings, paths that doubled back, rustlings in the undergrowth.

'A spine-chilling howl was heard. Desmond felt the hairs on the back of his neck stand up. He heard the patter of feet on the leaves . . .'

'Do shut up, Patricia,' Desmond said.

'Patricia. Do not tease your brother.'

'Honestly, Mother, you're all such stick-in-the-muds. Dessie can stand up for himself, can't you, Desmond?'

'I wish your father would take a firmer line with you, Patricia,' Doris said.

'He would need to get home a little earlier to take a firm line with me. I'll have to remind him in the morning.'

'You would do well to keep your mouth shut, hussy.' Doris had moved to the unlit niche beside the fireplace. It felt like a moment foretold. Something that went back into the history of story. A fireside gathering joined by a stranger, a teller of arcane tales, travellers fearing to look into the darkness beyond the firelight where the stranger stood.

'Mother, please,' Desmond said.

'And you who think yourself the head of wit. A gawk stood on a street corner handing out tracts to those more witless than yourself.'

Ferguson saw Desmond look at Patricia. *This has happened before.* Patricia got to her feet and ran lightly to her mother, silk pumps on her feet under the robe like some slippered princess. She took her mother by the hands as if she would lead her into the light.

'Come upstairs, Mother, I'll brush your hair. You like that.'

'Did I not say to keep your mouth shut? Mouth and legs shut is the way of it for a lass around here.'

'Upstairs now, Dorrie Curran. It's getting cold in here,' Patricia said. Doris's face was in darkness but Ferguson saw her bearing change, a masculine stance, an air of someone who would command the shadows, would gather them about. Desmond stood beside the fire while Patricia uttered little noises of cajoling, of comfort and drawing out. When she at last brought Doris into the firelight her mother's hair hung around her face and she moved like a frail elder, waving her hands blindly in front of her. Patricia held her hand. Desmond took her elbow and they moved her to the door and into the hallway beyond. The door closed, leaving Ferguson alone in the drawing room to wonder if this outlandish processional had taken place.

Ferguson waited for Curran until just before twelve. The fire went down. Ferguson could hear voices upstairs but could not make out what they were saying, offstage reckonings and shiftings. As the night went on the voices became more indistinct.

Although he knew the Currans were still there, the house began to feel empty, the voices like something out of the past, the voices of ancient summonings. He wondered how old the house was. In olden days was there the brush of crinolines in unfurnished drawing rooms? The electricity wavered and almost went out.

Ferguson closed the door behind him and lit a cigarette. As he opened the car door he heard feet on the gravel behind him. He turned quickly to see Patricia. She was bare-legged, wearing a belted raincoat.

'Christ,' he said.

'I didn't mean to frighten you,' Patricia said. 'I came out for a smoke. Mother doesn't agree. I hid my cigs in the laundry but I think she must have found them and thrown them out.'

'She's right. You shouldn't be smoking.'

'Don't be such a hypocrite, Harry. Let me have a pull of yours.' She leaned forward and took the cigarette from his hand.

'I don't think your father would approve.'

'Father doesn't approve of much, really. Besides, we smoke all the time in school.'

'I'm surprised they let you.'

'They don't know. We do it in the lavatories.'

The lore of illicit cigarettes, schoolgirls clustered in the cubicles, the quick shared drags, butts nipped to a duck's arse. Toilet-door graffiti and drawings, inked-in and smutty, genitalia outlined in pen, scribbled pubes.

'I'm sorry about Mother.'

'I know that her nerves trouble her, Patricia.'

'Her language was atrocious.'

'I've heard worse.'

'So have I, Harry.'

Patricia leaned forward and took the cigarette from his hand. She inhaled and held the smoke, a faraway look on her face as though she considered the substance of it. She exhaled, the smoke hanging in the night air, then handed the cigarette back to him, the butt dampish, lipstick on it.

'Thank you, Harry. You won't tell Father, will you?' she said, putting her hand on his arm for a moment. Ferguson tried to remember the last time he had stood like this with a woman, close enough to be aware of her warmth, lost in her meaning touches.

'I better go,' he said. She leaned forward and he could feel the length of her body against his, a thoughtful look on her face, a kind of carnal fathoming. Her lips touched his cheek and then she was gone into the night. Ferguson looked up. He thought he saw a curtain move in an upstairs window. He ground the cigarette into the gravel and got into the car.

At Whiteabbey he saw headlights coming along the lough shore. He stopped his car and got out. The Attorney General's black Lancia, travelling fast. The speeding car itself like bad tiding in transit through the night, the paintwork gleaming, a glimpse of the attorney's face set hard and tight-lipped. Ferguson wondering if he had been called home from gaming to deal with his wife.

Curran slowed when he saw Ferguson's car. He parked at the sea wall and crossed the road.

'There's been a killing,' Ferguson said.

'I heard.'

'Some pup called Taylor from the Shankill murdered a woman by the name of McGowan in Newington. If we convict

Taylor we'll have to hang him. The town will go up in flames. Therefore there won't be a guilty verdict. There's a couple of prosecutors in your office will take it on. Old hands. They'll put up a show of a fight and take a swan dive at the end. Justice is seen to be done. Taylor walks in the end.'

'I'm going to take the case myself.'

'Are you sure you want to do that? The Attorney General shouldn't be dirtying his hands with this. The world and his mother knows that Taylor done it. It won't look good. The Attorney throwing a case.'

'I don't intend to throw it. I intend to win it.'

'Win it? You can't convict Taylor and hope to build a political career in the province,' Ferguson said. 'The mob won't have it and the bar won't have it.'

'What odds would you give, Ferguson, that I can prosecute Taylor, win the case and then join the High Court as a judge?'

'No odds at all, Mr Curran. I'd give you no odds at all.'

'What was the character of the dead woman?'

'Respectable Roman Catholic, given to the telling of her beads, statues, mass, the whole papish lot.'

'The defendant?'

'A bad lot. In and out of employment. Lightfingered by the sound of it. His girlfriend was in the family way and he was due to marry her a few days after the murder. He was asking around the town if he could borrow money.'

'Guilty then?'

'As sin.'

'And is it not my job to chastise sinners?'

'Let God look after his sins. We'll look after the city.'

'I'm going to convict him, Harry.'

'Then it's a long haul to the judge's bench.'

'Do you remember when we met, Harry? We took that seat against the odds, didn't we?'

'There's odds and there's odds, Mr Curran. You've dealt me a bad hand here.'

'It's not the hand, Harry, it's how the cards are played.'

Two

OCTOBER 1947

Two years earlier Ferguson had been at the bar of the Reform Club when Curran brought his wife home from London. Curran wearing evening dress, Doris in a red satin gown. The Melody Aces were playing Tommy Dorsey in the ballroom. Curran leading her to their table. Bringing that feel of post-war London to the room. Doris smoking Black Cats in a cigarette holder. She had her hair up and her shoulders were bare. She used her hands when she talked, something that Ferguson would notice in her daughter. Jerky, edge-of-control gestures.

'Curran got a live one,' Ellis Harvey said. 'He's the coming man.' Harvey was the election officer for the city ward. He was a tall man with long strands of hair wrapped around his head. He stooped over people as though a visitant come to lay claim to their soul. He worked as a keeper of Egyptian antiquities in the Ulster Museum. Ferguson thought of him at night, among the pottery shards and scarabs, the godless anubi.

'You've got a seat lined up for him?'

'He lined up his own damn seat. And now I need an election agent for him.'

'Who's that?'

'You, Harry.'

'No.'

'It's about time you got your feet wet.'

'I'm doing all right.'

'You're a scholarship boy trying to make it in a public-school world. Don't get me wrong, Harry. I admire your brain. But you need somebody to attach yourself to. You could be running this town. And between ourselves, his nibs needs a minder.'

'Curran? Why?'

'He's a fondness for the card table. And the horses too. In fact my information is that Curran would bet on two flies walking up a wall. Men like that think they're in control. But they come a cropper in the end. That's where you'll be needed, Harry. Let me introduce you.'

'He won't want somebody like me.'

'There's one thing about Lance Curran. He's no snob. He looks down on all of us, no matter what tie we have on. Lance Curran will want you. You grew up on the streets and you know them. You're smart and you're discreet. I've already told him about you.'

They walked over to Curran. Curran stood to shake Ferguson's hand. Ferguson wearing a Burton suit, brown loafers. Curran in starched shirt front and collar, shaking his hand and holding it for a minute.

'You're from Cambrai Street,' Curran said.

'That's right.' The shipyard. Neat brick housing. His father a riveter. A man who fixed things in his shed, who made things solid in the world.

'My husband likes to know where people are from.' Doris Curran stretched out her hand. She was wearing satin gloves to the elbow. 'Sit here beside me, Mr Ferguson. I haven't made many friends here yet. You can tell me stories. There must be stories about this place.'

'Lots, Mrs Curran.'

'Lance said you might be working with him. That would be wonderful. You can work with us for ever. We'll call you Harry and when we're old you can come around and drink sherry in the conservatory.'

Doris keeping up the conversation. Easy company. She had a son, Desmond. She had a daughter, Patricia. She talked about the early years. Their childhood something she had fallen through, a place of dark wonders. Desmond the golden one. A boy who read Greek. Who made model aircraft from balsa and fragrant glues. A boy who came home one day with a cracked plaster statue of a saint and put it on the windowsill of his room and asked his mother if she would like to pray.

Ferguson asked her about Patricia. She had no respect for her mother's things. Patricia had taken out her best Linton china and used it for a dolls' tea party. She had used a silk Hermès scarf to tie a doll to the swing in the garden. She had no idea what possessions meant to a married wife. How they were to be set aside and cherished. Patricia was a sly prattler. A pincher of flesh. When she was small she lifted the poker from the fire and put it to her brother's bare leg to see what would happen.

Doris asked about Ferguson. If his parents were proud of him, if he had a special girl. She had a way of touching you when she spoke, twisting her hands in awkward shapes and placing them against a lapel or a sleeve. Speaking in breathy asides, all tics and nervous gestures. But Ferguson sensed stillness. Something behind her eyes, a wary presence, a watcher in the shadows.

'Lance doesn't like me to say it, but I was brought up in the loony bin. Broadmoor. People always laugh at that. You're not laughing, Harry.'

'I only laugh when something is funny, Mrs Curran.'

'My father was the superintendent.'

'You could learn a lot in a place like that.'

'I'm not sure if you learn good things. Them is places of wickedness.' Ferguson looked at her, but she had turned away from him. *Them is places of wickedness.* Something askew in the phrasing. The watcher in her eyes.

'A ladies' choice, Mr Ferguson. Shall we dance?'

They took to the floor, and Ferguson thinking back to that night would wonder if everything that took place afterwards had been foreseen by Curran or read by him in the stars, Doris remote and precise in his arms. They danced, seeing themselves in the gilt-mirrored walls, dancing through their own ruin in an iron gavotte.

Curran touched Ferguson's sleeve.

'Do you play billiards, Mr Ferguson?'

'Snooker.'

'Come with me.' Curran led him up a narrow staircase. The billiard room was on the top storey of the club, built into the peaks of the roof. There were four tables in the room, each with its own lit canopy. They were the only players. There were brass counting frames on the wall and the scrolled names of members. In the dim light of the tables these were the devices of a closed society.

'What do you have in your wallet, Mr Ferguson?'

'What?'

'Money. What money do you have on your person?'

'Fifty pounds.' Curran raised an eyebrow. 'A client's money,'

Ferguson said, 'he's to be paid tomorrow.'

'I'll match it. A single game. Winner takes all.'

'You know what might happen, Mr Curran, if I bet a client's money and lose it?'

'If there is no wager then there is no game. I'm not playing for your client. Or for you, Harry. I'm not playing for consequences. I'm playing for money. Are you in?'

'I'm in.'

'You're a gambler, then.'

'I wouldn't say that.'

'A player, then.'

'Yes. A player.'

Ferguson had grown up near the Jampot snooker hall. He was good at the game. He'd played adults when he was a teenager, carrying his own cue from home. Nodding to the man at the door, walking into the club on the balls of his feet, seeing himself as clear-eyed and dextrous, no heir to these men in work boots and caps bent to their task under the tasselled lights, studying the table, the green baize cloth etched with blue chalklines. Cigarette smoke hanging in a canopy below the ceiling, the heavy roof trusses, men murmuring to each other and the noise of the tables, the ceramic report of ball against ball. Ferguson would sight along the cue and take his shot, leaving his cheek against the cue so that you could sense the movement of the ball through the cloth, the vibration on the slate base plate of the table, the deep soundings.

Ferguson greased his hair back and played with a cigarette hanging from the corner of his mouth. He started doing tricks and taking bets on them. Jump shots. Cueing behind his back.

Setting up complicated cannons that sent the ball around the table. He took on a man from the Shankill and racked up a sixteen red break against him for 147. He didn't see what was coming.

The hall was an extension of their workplace. These men revered objects that were machined to fine tolerances, hair's-breadth clearances. The table itself a matter of substance constructed in timber and brass. Things you could put your hand to. They saw Ferguson as slick, circling the table with his hustler's gait.

The night after the 147 break he left the Jampot, walking home. A man he knew to see stopped him at the mouth of Thompson's entry. He asked Ferguson for a light. Ferguson palmed his Zippo and lit it, a kerosene tang hanging in the air.

'Tell us this, son,' the man said. 'Where did the last rivet in the Titanic go?'

Ferguson brought the lighter up to the man's face.

'I don't know,' he said.

The man touched his cigarette to the flame then hit Ferguson hard in the mouth. Ferguson fell to the ground. Two other men stepped out from behind him. One of them kicked him in the ribs. The other lifted the cue case, opened it and handed the two pieces to the first man. He broke each piece over his knee and threw them on the ground. He bent over Ferguson.

'In the last hole,' he said. 'The last fucking rivet in the Titanic went in the last fucking hole.'

'I haven't played for a few years,' Ferguson said.

'Your money,' Curran said.

Ferguson took the money from his inside jacket pocket. Five ten-pound notes. He put them on the edge of the table. Curran took a leather wallet from his coat and matched Ferguson's amount. He took a brass penny from his fob pocket and showed it to Ferguson. Ferguson called heads. Curran tossed the coin and it came up tails.

Curran smoothed the nap of the cloth and racked the balls. Ferguson set the brass scoreplate. Curran chalked the tip of his cue and broke the reds. They played the game without speaking, each man intent on his shot. Ferguson playing cautiously, building the shots, taking the easy colours and retreating into snookers, placing the white close to the cushion. Curran picking off difficult reds and going for the black, using the rest and the spider, taking the game to the limit every time. He refused an easy cut on the blue to the middle pocket, instead going for a cannon on the black, which he missed, leaving the pack of reds open. Ferguson took three reds, a yellow and a brown before he missed an easy pink, leaving Curran on the table again. Curran took the next red and a difficult black. He took a long red to the yellow pocket and screwed the cue ball back to leave him on the black. He drew ahead three times and each time refused the easy shot that would have finished the game.

At the finish the game was Curran's to take with a long black to the top right, the black resting against the cushion an inch from the pocket. Ferguson would have gone for a safety, played the percentages. He reckoned that Curran would try to cut it in. But Curran measured up a cannon from the far cushion.

'The white will go down,' Ferguson said. 'You'll forfeit the game.'

'I think it won't go,' Curran said.

'It's long odds that it won't,' Ferguson said. 'Cue ball to the middle pocket.'

Curran bent to the cue. He gave it heavy side. It struck the black, flighting it hard and true, but Ferguson wasn't watching the black. He knew the ball was on its way. He was watching the white cue ball, trying to judge its momentum as it curved across the table, still carrying spin from the side that Curran had put on it. They watched it stop in the jaws of the pocket, still spinning. Ferguson heard the black ball hit the leather backstrapping of the green pocket and drop into the net, the white still rotating on its axis and coming to a halt poised on the lip of the pocket.

'You win,' Ferguson said. Curran went to where the money had been placed on the edge of the table. He took his own fifty and put it back into his pocket. He held out his hand with Ferguson's £50 in it.

'Take it,' he said.

'What sort of man do you think I am?' Ferguson said.

'I think we have established that. Take the money. It's not a gift. It's a down payment for your services as an election agent. You'll have to earn it out.'

Curran placed the money beside Ferguson. He walked around the table and tapped the mahogany below the middle pocket once. The white ball fell into the netting with a soft sound.

'We've got work to do,' Curran said. He turned and left the room without looking back. Ferguson took the money from the table and put it back in his pocket. It was not money that had been wagered on the table that night and they both knew it.

Ferguson drove them to his office on the Shankill. The building had been a shirt factory. Ferguson's mother had worked there until her death and then his sister and he remembered the women at their machines, shoulder to shoulder. When the firm had closed Ferguson had entered with the bailiffs and served the notice to quit.

When the workers had been turned out, Ferguson had taken the manager's office. Curran kept pace with him as he climbed the wrought-iron staircase, the sound of their passage echoing in the unlit spaces of the factory floor. The shadow of presses and cutting tables below them in the dark. The building creaked, the heat of the day stored in its brickwork and timbers, the material shivering with their passing, a stirring in the unquiet dark. There seemed to be more shirts every time he passed through.

Curran knew the city wards and constituencies well. Knew the city in all its devising. Ferguson wasn't surprised to hear that Curran had chosen a marginal constituency that had been held by only a few votes in the last election. They sat until dawn working their way through the city boroughs, street by street. Ferguson working without a map, naming the shops and public houses, putting faces to the names, the profile of the area changing, whole populations on the move, the shifting masses, the gatherings and factions, the reeking shambles and spillover markets. Boundaries shifted, thoroughfares were erased. Curran didn't know the detail, couldn't put names to the streets, but he was able to read the maps, know what way the city was tending, what its future boundaries were.

'How?' Ferguson said.

'How?'

'You know the city but you don't know it.'

'I was in the air corps. We flew out of Sydenham. I know it from the air.'

'I see.'

'We have a lot to do, Harry.'

They worked on. Counting new votes and discarding old ones. Coming up short by one or two votes in each ward, seeing the seat slip away.

As the light came up Ferguson got to his feet and went to the window, looking out over the roofs of houses to the mountain behind the city.

'We're short seventy, maybe eighty,' he said. 'Even at that you'll have to work every vote. You need to be out at every church gate, every fete and funeral. You'll have to do the revival meetings and the dog tracks.'

'I'll do what I have to do,' Curran said. 'As will you, Harry.'

'Come to the window,' Ferguson said. Curran stood and came to the window.

'There,' Ferguson said, 'can you see the patch of green over there, and that one?' Look like parks?'

'There are no parks up there.'

'No. City never seen fit to build them. But they're open spaces nevertheless.'

'I can see that.' Curran plotting the city in his head, airborne, looking for the green spaces, the phantom parklands. 'Milltown,' he said, 'Milltown and Dundonald. The cemeteries.'

'That's right. The cemeteries. We take a roll call of Milltown. The deceased might have finished with life but it hasn't finished with them. We register them, as many as we need, and then they vote. You'll have your seat, Mr Curran.'

Curran went to the table. He rolled up Ferguson's map and put it under his arm, then turned to him.

'This conversation didn't take place, Harry.' Curran did not look back. Ferguson heard his footsteps on the metal stairway. Ferguson unlocked a metal filing cabinet and took out a hard-back account book titled 'Ratepayers, Deceased'. He had drawn the boundary of his bond with Curran and now set ghosts to patrol it. He reflected that Curran had got good value for his £50. He opened the book in front of him and bent to his ledger of the dead.

Three

APRIL 1949

The accused, Robert Taylor, was being held at Glenravel Street RUC barracks. Ferguson and his wife Esther drove down the Antrim Road into the city centre.

'Did he do it?' Esther asked.

'I'd say so,' Ferguson said.

'That poor woman.' Esther looked out of the window. 'He'll get off with it, won't he?'

'Why do you say that?'

'The people that run this city. They won't let one of their own be convicted for something like this.'

'I believe that in certain American states, a white man will not hang for the murder of a Negro. In some places I believe it is considered a misdemeanour.'

'They'll let the same thing happen here. You will, I should say.'

'Am I one of them, Esther?'

'Of course you are, Harry.'

Carlisle Circus was empty. A Crossley tender was parked beside the entrance to the New Lodge Road. Evening in the city. Ferguson turned towards the city centre.

'What will happen, Harry?'

'They'll find a reason not to proceed to trial. The waters will be muddied. Besides, a jury will never convict in this town. Not for murdering a papist.' Ferguson felt her shudder.

Ferguson stopped outside North Queen Street RUC station. They waited in the evening silence. Ferguson could smell his wife's perfume. Schoolgirls in Methody uniforms crossed the street in front of them, then entered a side street and were gone, so that Ferguson wondered if he had in fact seen them or some phantasm of adolescence lost in the evening street.

Ferguson had met Esther at a tennis club dance at the boat club on the banks of the Lagan at Hay Island. Esther did not belong to the bare-legged athletic girls, their blonde hair shining as they gathered in the sunlight, intent, laughing, already fading into a history of midsummer evenings. Esther stayed at the bar all night. She was like a woman he had seen in films at the Curzon and the Vogue. The born to be bad and the gone to the bad. Trading come-hithers across downtown cocktail bars.

Three weeks after the dance Esther telephoned him from Larne. She said her sister had gone to London to work and had left her mansionette flat empty. The mansionettes stood on high ground overlooking the docks. They had stayed in the flat for three days. She would not be sated.

The mansionettes were now derelict. The facades had been left standing, roofless, the windows empty. Ferguson drove past them every evening. The dark houses of his desire.

'Will you wait in the car for me?' Ferguson said.

'I think I might walk as far as the Reform Club,' Esther said. She leaned over to him. He felt her light, dry-lipped kiss.

'They say that Taylor looks like Bobby Breen.' She opened her door and got out of the car.

'Who?'

'Bobby Breen. He was a child film star. Cheery and cheesy

with curly hair and a button nose. Sang as well. A child soprano.'

'That's all I need.'

'You remember the song. It was on the radio all the time.'

'No, I don't remember.'

'It's a Sin to Tell a Lie.' Esther bending down to tell him, then walking away from him towards the Fountain, towards Royal Avenue and the Reform Club.

Inspector McConnell was waiting for him at the reception desk of the police station. There were uniformed policemen with Lee-Enfields at the front door and at the entrance to the cell block and Ferguson noted that they had chosen positions which commanded a field of fire the length of the stuccoed hallway. The men regarded him without expression. They had stood this way through riot and pogrom. At their posts throughout the empire. Night's constables holding the line. 'They'll not spring him with them boys keeping watch,' McConnell said.

'Will they try?' Ferguson said.

'They'd haul him out and shoulder him down the Shankill Road if they could get at him. They would carry him and proclaim the glory of the lord,' McConnell said. 'My men have orders to plug the first bastard comes through that door.'

'Bail?'

'The bloody magistrate near gave it to him. DPP opposed. Had to tell the beak there'd be civil war out there if he walked free.'

Ferguson knew the thinking. Another one gone and all to the good. But you had to watch out for civil unrest. Men gathering in the margins of old battlegrounds, the Brickfields,

Smithfield, hands in pockets, waiting for dark.

McConnell took him down a distempered brick corridor to the cells. Ferguson had been here before. He had been duty solicitor when the Negro soldier Wiley Harris had been arrested for the murder of Harry Coogan. The soldier haggling over price with the pimp then stabbing him. The bored girl waiting in the bomb shelter, bargained over, the pimp's reward a knife in the guts under a gibbet moon. Harris sitting quietly in the cell, wearing USAAF fatigues, his hands between his knees.

'Did you do it?' Ferguson had asked.

'Does it matter if I did, sir? I'm in trouble anyway.'

'You're in the right place for trouble.'

'Same as the place I came from. Exact same.'

'Taylor's in cell eight, sir,' the sergeant in charge said.

'What's your impression, sergeant?' Ferguson said.

'If wrong had a human form, I'd say it's sat behind that door, Mr Ferguson.'

The gaoler opened the cell door and Ferguson stepped inside, stooping a little. Taylor stood in the middle of the cell so that the evening sun shone on him. Ferguson remembered what Esther had said about Bobby Breen. Taylor had wavy brown hair, parted on the right, the button nose, the cheery demeanour. *A low-rent Fauntleroy*, Ferguson thought. *Babyface killer.*

'Are you with the police?' Taylor said.

'My name's Harry Ferguson.'

'Do I not get to pick my own solicitor?'

'Not unless you got plenty of money.'

'They say I'm going to need a hotshot.'

'Who says that?'

'The peelers. Them boys out there.'

'Never mind what they say. I want you to tell me what happened.'

'It's all a mistake, Harry. I never went next nor near that woman.'

'Did you know her?'

'I done work for her when I worked for Barrett the painter. She was dry as a bone and mean to boot.'

'Did you go to her house yesterday afternoon?'

'Like fuck I did.'

'I'll take that as a no. Did you go to her house at any other time after you worked for Barrett?'

'I'm supposed to be getting married, Harry. I was looking for a bit of work, there's no crime in that.'

'You asked Mrs McGowan for work?'

'You might as well ask that wall for a chance in life as talk to her.'

'And she turned you down.'

'I'm as good as the next man when it comes to a brush.'

'That's all I want to know for the moment.' Ferguson rose to go.

'Hang on a second, Harry, you going to leave me here? What about bail?'

'You'll be back in the magistrates' court on Monday. They'll talk about bail then.'

'I was supposed to be getting married on Monday.'

'Is that right. Wedding all paid for?'

'That's for me to know and you to find out.'

'I've questioned better men than you, son.'

Ferguson had served as a legal officer for the occupying powers after the war, conducting interrogations at Nuremberg prison. A place of dark pine trees and snow-filled approaches. He had been present at the interrogation of Rudolf Hess and other high-ranking officers. Blond, insolent. He had taken depositions which were later presented at the Nuremberg tribunals. At night he read transcripts of atrocity. He felt himself alone with the almanacs of the damned. He entered the prison at night and left it before dawn. Although there was the appearance of law he well knew what process was set in train here and to what end it led.

'You're a sly dog, Harry.' Taylor got up and walked up to Ferguson. He took his lapel between his finger and thumb and rubbed it gently. 'You think I done her for the money? Not true. No way José. I was getting fifteen pound last night as a loan from a friend. That was to pay for the nuptials.'

Ferguson took a step back. Away from the freckles. The earnest man-boy eyes. Fixed in the forty-watt low-fidelity light of gaolhouse candour. Ferguson knew the sergeant in charge was watching them through the peephole. *If wrong had a human form.*

'Nice piece of herringbone,' Taylor said, 'nice piece of cloth in the jacket.' Ferguson took his hand away and knocked on the door. The duty sergeant opened it.

'Mr Lunn's in station reception,' he said. Ferguson nodded. Lunn would want to be Taylor's solicitor. He followed the sergeant, the man's hobnail boots loud on the parquetry. Lunn stood in the middle of the floor. He was a tall florid man with small eyes, a backstreet opportunist, rabble-rouser and slum leaseholder.

'Harry,' Lunn said, his eyes narrowing, 'I didn't think I'd find you here.'

Ferguson nodded to him and sat down on a wooden bench that stood along the wall.

'Lunn.'

'Curran's going to prosecute Mr Taylor.'

'That's right.'

'He'll go in with kid gloves.'

'Curran will do what he wants to do.'

'He's an ambitious man, Harry. He'll put up a bit of a show and then throw in the towel.'

'That sounds a bit like an instruction to me.'

'Take it any way you like, Harry. The truth of the matter is that the mob will decide what happens. They always do.'

'What about the judge and jury?'

'You're a comedian, Ferguson. I didn't know that about you. Your sense of humour escaped my notice so far. Why do you think there's men standing here with guns? You think it's because the mob will try to punish Taylor? They'd carry him out of here shoulder high if they were let. You know it and Curran knows it and if he goes for a guilty verdict he might as well pack his bags.'

'I'm not here to tell Mr Curran what to do.'

'No you're not. That's for sure and certain. You're Curran's dog is what you are. When he says tail you start wagging. When he says bite somebody in this town gets bit.'

Lunn pushed past the sergeant in charge and descended towards the cells.

'He'll meet his match with that boy', the sergeant said. 'The harm of the world is in him.'

On the 14th of July 1949 twenty-seven-year-old Robert Taylor was charged with the murder of forty-nine-year-old Mary McGowan. It was alleged that Taylor had entered Mrs McGowan's house at 18 Ponsonby Avenue, on the pretence of using the telephone. He had previously been part of a Barretts of Sunnyside Street crew painting the house, so Mrs McGowan wasn't suspicious when he came to the door. The prosecution stated that Taylor had choked Mrs McGowan with a cord, beaten and stabbed her, then poured hot soup over her.

Despite her injuries, Mrs McGowan had retained consciousness for two days. On six separate occasions she identified 'Robert the Painter' as the man who had attacked her.

It was alleged that Taylor was looking for money. He was due to be married to his pregnant girlfriend three days after the crime and he had gambled away the money he needed to pay for the wedding. He had made several attempts to borrow money from friends and associates without success.

Although the victim had identified him as a painter who had worked on the house in Newington eight months previously, Taylor maintained that he had not been in the area since.

The names. Newington. Ponsonby. The aspirant classes. The grid of streets. Neat between-the-wars housing. They had raised themselves above the darkness. The murder seen in the context of political unrest. The city had a history of pogrom, murder and arson, the handed-down rancours of the age. Factions did battle in the streets. Preachers stood on street corners, kin to the ranters of old. There were boilermakers, keel-layers, riveters. They thought in tonnages, vast displacements. There was God in these things. They wanted it known that these were works of the imagination, the wrought matter of the mind.

The courthouse faced the Crumlin Road jail, its basalt slabs carted from the quarries of the black mountain to the north of the city. An underground passage led from the gaol to the courthouse. In all thirteen prisoners were hanged in Crumlin Road. They were interred in the prison yard. Their names and dates of execution were etched on the wall congruent to their burial place. Taylor was to be represented by Robert Hanna QC, Mr Justice Sheil presiding. The prosecuting counsel was named as Attorney General Lancelot Curran QC.

Four

Taylor had a 'box of tricks' he kept in the shed. It was an old ammunition box, its green paint chipped in places. Taylor had stolen it from the back of a military truck at Magilligan camp. No one else was allowed to touch it. He kept his tools in it. Besides the tools there was a yellowing collection of pornography that he'd found in a service shelter at the waterworks. Girls in marcelled curls wearing bathing suits, striking kittenish poses at the front of the pile, then working back towards what Taylor called the hard stuff. The smudged monochromes, the torn-out magazine pages. Girls who knew what was what, legs akimbo. Starlets with a small-town intentness about them. The way they looked at the camera. Where they'd come from. Knowing the shadows out there, the haunted spaces, what lay in the dark beyond the suburban lawns.

The men had slicked-back hair and small moustaches. They had a spivvish, across-the-border look to them. Taylor tried to copy the way they looked. He bought a double-breasted suit at Burton and wore it to the dogs at Celtic Park. He liked to get down among the dogs, the wet ash smell of the cinder track, the dogs muzzled, straining. The trainers muscling the dogs, working back from the shoulders, the spavined-looking ribs sticking out to give the greyhounds a slum-dog look, skulking in the noon heat. Taylor would run his hand along their backs feeling the vertebrae through the fine-haired pelt, and the heat. Taylor bet on horses and football, but most of all on the dogs. There was a cruel look to them, remorseless. He liked the moment when the traps opened and the greyhounds left the hutches, changed into something else, the pattered salvo of their paws, kicking up sand pulses, the lithe footfall. Taylor thought about bloodhounds in films given a piece of the victim's clothing to smell, working their way through the swampland, torches swinging from side to side, a mournful baying.

Taylor was known as Robert the Painter. Paint was his medium. He was familiar with its qualities of camouflage, of deception. He was always in the shed, mixing paints, trying out colours on the walls. Carmine, turpentine and linseed oil. He painted his parents' sitting room five or six times a year. He could never leave things alone. He met Lily when he was painting her sister's kitchen.

Robert took Lily to the pictures. He said he was a foreman at Barrett's painting firm. He told her about the things he took from houses he worked in. Ornaments and pieces of delft. He told her about the paint that was made from insect wings. He told her about the pigment made from ground-up poppies. When she took out her make-up he touched it, rubbing it between his fingers, tasting it. He'd touch her between her legs and put his fingers to his lips.

It was all about surfaces. Glazes and washes. He showed her how to cut in with the brush, work the paint into the plaster.

Taylor took her to the parks at night. Lady Dixon's and Botanic. They'd climb over the fence. He'd back her up against the glass of the palm house. Taylor always looking for the textures in things. The silks, the nylon. He'd pull her stocking over his hand, smell it.

She always had to plead with him. He was always overstepping the mark. He named other girls who had let him touch their breasts, their silky thighs. Who had let him put his hand down there. He told her that it was normal. They all did it. They all sighed and turned their heads away on the damp grass.

'Don't, Robert, it's not safe.'

'You want it. You all want it.' Robert's manifesto. He said that he could be a great artist if he put his mind to it. Robert took her to the dances in Maxim's. In the summertime they went to Bangor to the amusements. Robert would take her on the dodgems. He would belt her in, all little touches and smoothing her clothing down, arranging her skirt on her thighs, positioning the seatbelt over her breasts. Robert would take the wheel, blue sparks cascading from the grid. The careen and trundle of the dodgem-car bogies on the rubber matting. Robert would go the wrong way around the track. He saw her looking at the youth who attended the cars, setting them straight, stepping from car to car, crouching to turn the wheel. His hard-nosed road grace.

He played the horse track, betting on the coloured tin horses inching around the track. When he won he couldn't wait. He'd take her down an alley, in behind a pile of beer crates. He'd back her up against a wall, working at her. His tongue hanging out for it.

He would try to win at the rifle range but he always missed. She tried to pull him away but he wouldn't budge. He spent all of his money. He told the man behind the counter that the sights of the rifle were bent.

Taylor would be in a bad mood then. He could be spiteful. There would be pinches, an arm painfully gripped, hurtful pettings that left her sore and breathless. Taylor shifting the blame to her. I nearly had the bullseye but you jogged my elbow. You were sniffing and I couldn't concentrate.

In March Taylor took Lily to the greyhounds. She thought the greyhounds looked like wild creatures, amoral skulking things. Hunting dogs prowling in the shadowed area under the stand. When the hare was released she put her hand to her mouth, willing it around the stadium.

'It's only a bit of fur and metal,' Taylor said. 'The dogs'll do it no harm.' But Lily could see in their eyes what they were. Taylor took her to the top bar above the stands. The drinks were more expensive here but Taylor liked the swank, the ladies in fur coats, the men well got in Aquascutum coats and bespoke suits. Taylor felt that he belonged here. He bought a Babycham for Lily but she didn't drink it. She was pale and everything felt far away. Another race had started. Through the rain-streaked glass she saw the people stand to urge on the dogs but they were blurred and soundless, a ghost citizenry under the dog-track lights.

'You're pregnant, aren't you?' Taylor was staring at her hard. 'You're up the fucking bubble.'

People had difficulty believing that Taylor could have committed such a brutal murder. He was a slight, boyish figure. He had unruly red hair, parted at the side, green eyes, a button nose, an irrepressible smile. People called 'Bobby Breen' after him in the street.

SEPTEMBER 1925

Doris met Lance Curran at a tea dance at the Savoy Hotel. She danced with him three times. She wore a dress she had made herself from a pattern in Vogue magazine. The dress pattern came with dance steps. The dance steps were a sheet of paper you laid out on the floor with each step marked out with footprints. You placed your foot in each print and that showed you the step. That was how Doris learned to dance. Doris and Lance were photographed during an interval in the dancing. Pre-war glamours cling to them. Lance is wearing an evening suit. Doris's hair is arranged in a French bun. She is wearing gloves to her elbows. Lance is leaning back in his chair, a cigarette in his left hand, a glass on the table. He is a young man. He sees himself as without peer but she looks uncertain, as though she senses the catastrophe that her life will be. The onset of madness. Her daughter slain. Her son turned towards the light of God.

A cinema programme lies on the table between them. The film is Their Own Desire with Norma Shearer and Robert Montgomery. Shearer and Montgomery dance together in an early scene. Shearer is wearing an ankle-length chiffon dress. They dance a Charleston. The dance is highly stylised. The woman places her left hand high on the man's shoulder and he places his right hand in the small of her back, supporting her forearm so that she is forced to stand close to him, her pelvis pressed against his hip. He extends his left arm and holds it so that she must reach for it, his elbow high and crooked. She must raise her head sharply to look up at her partner. The camera pulls out to show that they are dancing among many other couples. The man fixed and stiff, forced into the mechanics of the dance, the woman forever looking up at him.

Men in uniform watch her and they ask her to dance. They know that war is coming. She finds herself circling the dance hall in the arms of provincial debonairs, Lance watching without expression. Lance takes her in his arms again and they dance against the mirrors until they seem lost among dozens of dancing couples. Each man in evening dress. Each woman wearing a long silk gown. The music drives them on. A masque of predation and desire.

On her way to the Savoy Doris saw a poster for Their Own Desire and regretted that she had not seen it. Lance insisted that they see it at the Odeon in Leicester Square. They stood in the queue, Lance wearing his overcoat and black evening suit, Doris in gown and gloves.

They sat in the balcony. You could hear the sounds that couples made in the back seats. The whispers and the shiftings. She wished that Lance would put his arm around her but he sat straight as a rod, the way he always did. Montgomery looks down at Shearer. Have you ever been kissed, he asks her, and Doris knew that he didn't mean kissed. Montgomery and Shearer danced together to Blue Is the Night. From the back seats of the cinema a woman moaned as though she had sought to confirm all that she was in the dark but had instead found something desolate there.

When they came out of the cinema the wind funnelled down the streets, making the glass shopfronts shiver. A few people moved quickly out of the station and disappeared, driven before the storm. Lance stood at the top of the station steps, his black coat flowing out behind him. He looked as if he had summoned the storm. The night was full of wrath and he was its master.

Lance takes Doris to the jazz clubs and she wonders how he knows about them. The Black Cat. The Boom Boom Rooms. There are black marketeers there, foreign hostesses. She sits in low-ceilinged rooms listening to Negro musicians. When they walk through the West End and Soho the club callers and toms call out to him as he passes, falling silent when they see Doris. Lance knows the gaming clubs. She watches as he plays cribbage, gin and euchre. There are games of sheepshead and pinochle run by demobbed American servicemen. Seven-card stud and Texas hold 'em. There is a sense of desolate one-street towns about the players. Games of the prairie darkness.

In October Lance drove Doris to Feltwell airfield. There were mechanics in overalls working on the machines. The Bristol had RAF roundels on the wings. Lance walked Doris around the aircraft. It smelt of epoxies, clear varnishes. The wing canvas on balsa stretchers. Workshop scents. Doris was afraid to fly but Lance talked about how it felt, being aloft, buffeted. The far-from-the-ground possibilities that opened up on the edge of a weather system.

He placed a leather helmet on her head and arranged it. Thirty years later she heard how he had placed a square of black silk on his head to pronounce the death sentence on Robert McGladdery and this moment came back to her, Lance setting the helmet, working at the chin straps, arranging the goggles on her forehead. Doris's hair was marcel-waved. The helmet would flatten it.

'I'll look a fright when I take it off,' she said, 'a perfect fright.'

She had worn jodhpurs and a short riding coat. One of the mechanics held out a leather flying jacket and she put it on. Lance zipped it, pulled it tight around her, cinched the waist belt.

'There's a bit of a squall coming, sir,' one of the mechanics said. 'I wouldn't go up if I were you.'

As the Bristol cleared the treeline, Lance turned to her and pointed to the sky behind the hangars. Across the flat washes and drained tidal fields a black cloud ran from horizon to horizon, its dense top rift with anvil lightning. The lightning cast light across the salt bents and derelict flax pits and the black cloud bore down on the scattering of homesteads and the huts of itinerant eelfishers.

The biplane gained altitude as though it would run before the storm. Then Doris felt it bank to port. She could feel the flex of the airframe, the wind risen to a shriek in the wing struts. Lance turned back from the front cockpit to look at her. His face was streaked with oil. He turned away and steered the Bristol towards the heart of the storm.

It came to her crouched in the rear of the aircraft how men played at forfeits and that what they wagered was often not their own to dispose of. She pulled the webbed strapping tight about her and awaited the storm.

The first buffetings she thought would unpick the fabric of the aircraft. The cloud was rent with updraughts and vortices and the wind roared so that cold voices gave tongue. Hailstones dashed upon the fabric of the aeroplane. One struck her goggles and starred the glass in the left eye and ice gathered in the folds of the leather jacket. Pale fire ran along the wing edges. The canvas snapped and the wing stretchers groaned. At the height of the storm Lance turned to look at her again. His face and goggles were covered with oil. There was blood on his cheek. Doris realised then that she would never know him.

Doris and Lance were married three months later in the registry office on the Strand. Lance wore his uniform as a reserve lieutenant in the Royal Ulster Rifles. She married Lance without knowing him. He was handsome and severe with that mouth that turned down at the corners. Desmond was born in 1926. Patricia was born in March 1933 in London. In November 1940 Lance went to the war.

Five

SATURDAY 16TH APRIL 1949

A still temperate day, the thermometer at seventeen degrees. Mary McGowan walked to the greengrocer's on Atlantic Avenue and back again. Courtesies were exchanged with neighbours. Mary wearing a knee-length tweed skirt and brown silk blouse edged in white lace, buttoned to the neck with a relief brooch at the collar. Mary knowing what was required. Orders totted, goods weighed out. You watched the scales and took nothing for granted.

Mary hadn't liked Taylor. He had worked at 18 Ponsonby Avenue the previous October as part of a painting crew from Barrett's of Sunnyside Street. In February 1949 he had returned to the house. Mary's daughter Kathleen came to the door. Taylor said that he had finished his apprenticeship and was setting up a painting business with his brother. Mary thanked him but said that she would keep her existing arrangement with Barrett. Taylor slammed the garden gate behind him.

It was about knowing what was important. There was a behind-the-lines feel to the day. Life going on. Hedges were being trimmed. Paintwork touched up. Mary bought bread from Kennedy's van. She crossed Atlantic Avenue to buy vegetables. As she emerged from the vegetable shop she was surprised to meet Taylor. He chatted to her about the weather. About the fact that her husband was in hospital, her daughter away for the day. Taylor was wearing a blue raincoat and light brown shoes, a colour that was described in court as 'light yellow'.

As Mary returned to Ponsonby Avenue Taylor walked in the opposite direction. When she was out of sight he turned right into Baltic Avenue and back on to Atlantic Avenue, entering the north end of Ponsonby Avenue.

Taylor was seen walking down Ponsonby Avenue by Mrs Shiels from number 28. The coat was belted and his collar was turned up. In the coat pocket he had a seven-foot length of strong twine, a seven-eighths spanner and a pair of gloves. Taylor stood out in the blue coat and yellow shoes. He looked as if he had wandered in out of some Middle European tale. A snatcher of children from folklore.

Mary McGowan's neighbour, John Lillis, greeted her as she returned home. Lillis was working in his front garden. The lilies were in bloom. The hollyhocks.

No matter how often it is presented, the witnessed day comes to you in fragments, drummed out in policeman's argot, legalities, coroner's reports, the talk of neighbours, the day's deep pathologies left in the details. The hollyhocks in bloom, the noontime trip to the shops. Foreboding creeping into the telling of it, sinister undertones. Mr Lillis staunched Mary McGowan's wounds after the attack. In the following years he was seen walking the streets after dark, his eyes fixed on the ground. His garden, left untended, became a wilderness.

Taylor knocked on the door of number 18. Mary came to the door. He asked her if he could use her telephone.

Number 18. A still interior. Things that are husbanded, tended to. Care is taken with the smallest of tasks. There are devotional images on the walls. A candle flickers. The household gods are watchful. There are delft ornaments and carnival-ware plates. These are the votives we set against the shadow within. The sun shone outside but in here you could almost believe that things were ordered differently. The interior shadowed with Romish leanings. Stories he'd heard as a child, priestholes, the furtive saying of masses, the soft chanting, the doctrinal taint.

Taylor couldn't stop himself from touching things as he followed Mary into the kitchen. She remembered that about him. Stroking the paintwork on the bannisters, fingering things, picking them up. Running his hand over the missal on the hall table, the foxed and worn leather cover, the beads handworn, venerated.

The only account of what happened in the house that morning came from dying statements from Mary McGowan and from the physical evidence at the scene. Taylor denied that he had been there at all.

It would appear that Mary turned her back on Taylor. He took the cord from his pocket and placed it around her neck, slipped the cord twice around her neck and tried to strangle her. Her breathing became laboured. She got her fingers between the cord and her flesh. She reached behind her with the other hand and scratched his face. Why would she not die?

She broke away from him. Bitch. She ran towards the kitchen. He struck her again and again with the spanner but it slipped from his grasp and Mary ran into the scullery. He struck her with a bottle of holy water. He stabbed her with a carving knife. Why would she not die? He punched her in the face. She fell to the ground but would not die. He kicked her in the back, in the face, in the kidneys. He went into the kitchen. There was a pot of soup on the stove. He carried the soup into the scullery and poured it over her and left her like that.

He went through her purse on the kitchen table. He found some coins. There were holy medals, scapulars. Faces watching him from Mary's holy pictures on the wall, brown-skinned men with high cheekbones and deep-set eyes. They made him nervous, their fierce hawklike gaze following him round the kitchen. Their minds honed by ordeal, alone in the desert reciting the names of God.

Taylor only found a few coins in Mary's purse. He went upstairs to her bedroom and began to empty drawers on to the floor. Somewhere there would be money, a roll of banknotes as thick as a clenched fist, bound with an elastic band like the ones that the bookies at Dunmore Park kept in their leather satchels. These people were bookmakers, publicans. Their bounty was solid, earthbound. They knew the value of cash. They knew the worth of things. Ferreting through drawers, the clothes and underthings, linens that had been given as wedding presents and were now kept pristine, the deep lode of constancy that ran through her life now unfolded and thrown aside.

Taylor froze when he heard the back door latch. He went to the window. Mary had got to her feet and staggered out into the back garden. She was first seen by two small boys. The Rafferty twins had been playing in their back garden at number 17 and had looked up to see Mary, blood-drenched and unrecognisable. The boys had heard of such apparitions in the schoolyard. They were seen as important figures of summoning. They lurked at night in tree-lined avenues. They haunted the waterworks, old hospital buildings, disused well shafts.

There was the Red Nurse. There was the One-Armed Man. The boys did not expect to see one of these figures in the back gardens of Ponsonby Avenue on a sunny morning. Mary's features were obscured by blood and swelling. An arm of her spectacles had lodged in her hair. The cord that had been used to strangle her hung around her neck. She made strange noises. The twins watched her in silence. They knew the rules. When Mr Skillen came round the corner the spell was lifted. Mary's arms made gestures of warding, of gathering. She stood alone in her own ghast lore. They ran into the house and told their mother there was a Red Lady in the garden.

No one saw Taylor leave the house. A storybook imp in a blue coat and yellow shoes skipping down Ponsonby Avenue past the lilies in bloom, the hollyhocks.

'What are these, Harry?' Esther languid on the settee, wearing a dressing gown.

'Jury lists.'

'What are they for?'

'The trial. Taylor.'

'You're going to try to get at the jury.'

'If they don't want people to see them, they shouldn't make the lists available.'

'What does Lance Curran think about this?'

'He doesn't know.'

'You're trying to make him lose his case. I thought you were his friend.'

'There's no friends in all of this. I'm on his side.'

'I don't understand.'

'If he loses the case he'll be seen as young, idealistic and wrong. He can survive that. If he wins it'll be seen as turning against his own side. Then he's finished.'

'I hate this life, Harry.'

'It's the only one I have.'

'I know. I'm going out later. I won't be in when you get back.'

'You never are.'

Ferguson walked down the path to his car. It was a still night. There was fog coming up from the river, an estuary murk carrying furnace smells from the shipyard, tar, hot rivets. There was a car parked further up the street, lights off, a man's shape in the front seat. Waiting for Esther perhaps. It was a night for assignations. There were wreathing vapours, couples looming out of the mist as though they took their substance and mystery from it.

Ferguson drove down Stranmillis Road to University Road. There were lights on in the law library. Desmond Curran was in his final year at the law faculty. 'It would appear', Curran said, 'that Desmond is more inclined to the law of Moses than the law of man.' Desmond Curran had taken to preaching and street leafleting in support of a Christian organisation called Moral Rearmament. Ferguson had received a call earlier that month to say that Desmond was leafleting outside the Dockers Club. Ferguson had sent two men to keep an eye on him. Ferguson had also reported back to Curran on Desmond's associates. Young men from the armed forces, loners, shy bespectacled students. Strays and hangers-on, Ferguson said.

On the road Ferguson stopped outside McKenzie's. Wine and Spirit Merchants in gilt lettering over the door. Polished brass on the window bars. Clientele from the shipyard and Mackie's foundry. McKenzie ran an undertaker's from the back of the premises. Ferguson had met him at political functions. McKenzie wore pinstripes, black patent shoes. He knew how the mob worked.

The drinkers at the bar watched Ferguson cross the floor. Foundry men taking in the creased raincoat, the scuff-marked brogues. Knew him for a fixer, one with the ward bosses and vote riggers and boundary men. Subalterns of corruption. The barman nodded him through the door behind the counter and down the stairs.

He found McKenzie in his workshop, stood in the middle of it in shirtsleeves, his jacket over the back of a chair. The air smelt of formaldehyde, wood shavings. The lights were low. Casket lids set against the wall in shadow. A half-finished coffin stood on trestles beside McKenzie. Ferguson tapped the side of it thoughtfully.

'Best red deal,' McKenzie said. 'I'll do you a price on one, Ferguson.'

'I'm not looking to use one for a while.'

'Neither was he.' McKenzie nodded to the adjunct room. A black tin coffin rested on the concrete floor. 'He was up on the ship gantry and a steel cradle collapsed above his head. Split the braincase wide open. You never know the day or the hour.'

McKenzie had been a street preacher but now he contented himself with his pub and his workshop with its congregation of shadows.

'The Lord giveth and the Lord taketh away,' Ferguson said, 'and in this case the Lord giveth you the chair of the jury in the Taylor case.'

'How do you know that?'

'You're on the jury. I want a not guilty verdict.'

'You want a lot. A child could see that Taylor killed the woman.'

'I still want a not guilty.'

'A hung jury's the best I can promise. If there was more I could give you I would. Taylor done us all a favour. One less to reckon with.'

'Does guilt or innocence come into it?'

'The woman paid down her tithe and went to what was prepared for her. The book speaks not of guilt or of innocence. The Lord will have what is his, day is day and night is night.' McKenzie reached into a drawer and pulled out a handful of frilled material.

'They will have this for to line their coffins, Mr Ferguson, to adorn them as they go before the light. But the Lord has no recourse to fripperies.'

'It's not fripperies I'm after, McKenzie. It's a good old-fashioned not guilty verdict.'

'This is a dead town, Ferguson. The citizens will go out of their mind over this.'

'That's why I want the verdict.'

'Is it? Who's representing the prosecution?'

'The Attorney General.'

'Lance Curran's prosecuting? What's your game, Ferguson? Lance Curran is your man. How come you're going against him?'

'None of your business, McKenzie. Will you do as you're bid?'

'I'll do what I can. That's all I can say. Now, I have a traveller to send on his way.'

Ferguson walked out into the night air. The fog was dense now. He pulled up the collar of his coat against the damp. The shadows gathered round. They were multitude.

Six

FEBRUARY 1961

The nurses told Ferguson that Doris looked forward to his visits. That she asked for the hairdresser each Wednesday, knowing that he would come on the Thursday morning, and did her make-up.

'I do believe she's a little bit soft on you,' the ward sister told Ferguson. 'She gets right and sharp if she's not looking the part on Thursdays.' The psychiatrist, Mr Brown, said that he believed Ferguson's visits were therapeutic and that it enabled her to anchor herself in the real world.

'That's a bit of a gag, Harry,' Esther had said, 'you being her anchor to the real world.'

'Not much of an anchor, is it?'

'Not much of a world.'

'Do you play bridge, Mr Ferguson?' Doris said.

'I never learned, Mrs Curran.'

'We used to play with the Buntings, and with the Donalds.'

'I believe it's a game of bluff,' Ferguson said.

'Yes,' Doris said, 'I was rather good at it.'

'So I've heard.'

'Did your wife play?'

'She isn't much good at bluffing,' Ferguson said. He got up

and went to the window.

'What is her name?'

'Esther.'

'I remember her now. She was a person of a nervous disposition. Not good for bridge. One needs to be fully in charge of one's emotions.'

Ferguson stayed at the window. The nurses said that Doris drifted in and out of personalities, inhabited and discarded them. The world in her head. The clamour of it. Minor royalty, street vendors, voices from her past, strangers wandering the psychic thoroughfares.

'Where is she now? Your wife?' Ferguson could see Doris reflected in the window, her head tilted back, a duchess, grace and favour dispensed.

'At home. She doesn't go out much.'

'Perhaps I should send Lucy to her.'

'Lucy?'

'The maid. A harmless-looking sort of a girl. She bears no resemblance to a murderer. None at all. I enquired of her how she found herself in Broadmoor here but she wouldn't tell me. Drowned her baby probably. That's what most of them are in for. Infanticide. The fruit of one's womb. Lucy's a cheery sort. Father says she keeps me out of mischief.'

The nurses said that Doris hid her medication. Hid it in her cheek and spat it out later. She was cunning. You had to keep your wits about you.

'Where are you now, Mrs Curran?'

'In Broadmoor Asylum for the Criminally Insane. Daddy is the superintendent. It's a very important job. Some of the best minds of a generation end up in here. The best sort of loony,

Lucy says. The very best sort of chaps.'

There was a small garden outside the window, enclosed by the hospital buildings. It was dark and muddy, the lawn trampled. Dusk was coming in from the lough and he remembered the night Patricia had been found on the driveway of the Glen. It had been such an evening, a drizzle that fell through nightfall and on into the dark of night as though it would never stop.

'Do you remember the night Patricia died, Mr Ferguson?'

'I do remember it, Mrs Curran.'

They had lifted Patricia from the wet ground. She was entitled to tenderness but received none. Her body was stiff and had to be forced into the back seat of the car. She was taken to the Whiteabbey surgery. She was laid out on the examining couch. Ferguson remembered the bloodless face. Thirty-seven stab wounds.

The place had been named Whiteabbey because the monks had worn white garments. The abbey was gone. The stones of it carted seaward to build the harbour. Esther had fancies of the monks abroad in the grounds of the Glen, tending still to some dark friary, their hooded faces, mendicant, unforgiving, adrift among the trees.

He had returned to the Glen and walked the murder site before the police arrived from the city. There was no blood. There were no drag marks. He had not seen Patricia's art folder, books and Juliet cap, although these items were later found at the scene, dry although it had rained all night. The rain pattered on dead leaves. He had felt himself in a story, lost, harried in a storybook forest. It had not occurred to him until then that Patricia's killer might still be in the trees. A face in the darkness, a watcher, pale and feral. He looked up towards the house. Through the bare, black branches of the trees he could see a light burning on the top storey of the house. A woman stood at the window, backlit, shadowed. He did not know if he was being watched or if the watcher had taken possession of the scene before her, a prioress of the dark and mistress of the night.

There was always the masque with the Currans. There was always the sense of dusty provincial theatrics, backstage intrigue, whisperings and gropings in the stalls. The frocktailed judge orchestrating proceedings.

Ferguson stood in the dark looking upward until he heard police sirens along the cold lough shore. The woman in the window lifted her arms above her head and brought the curtains together, the distant sirens her cold accolade.

'William Chester Minor.'

'I beg your pardon?'

'William Chester Minor. The surgeon of Crowthorne. He is incarcerated at her majesty's pleasure in Broadmoor.'

'I didn't realise.'

'He is a very intelligent man. My father spoke with him once or twice a week. He was batty though. He cut off his penis with a kitchen knife, Lucy told me. He put it in his pocket and walked around with it before he fainted from loss of blood.'

Ferguson took his hat from the chair in the corner of the room. He put on his overcoat and gloves.

'He left you too, didn't he?' Doris said.

'I beg your pardon?'

'Lance left you too. He took off to court and left us all here. You and I alone with the ghosts.'

*

Ferguson stood in the superintendent's office. The room was too warm. There was a smell of medicines in the air, an antiseptic reek. There was a notepad on the desk, leather-bound psychiatry books on the shelves. The superintendent was a balding man in his fifties. He wore corduroys and round glasses. He wished to be seen as eccentric. He had been to the higher reaches of consciousness and had not returned unchanged.

'How can I help you, Mr Ferguson?'

'Mrs Curran.'

'I can't discuss a patient's condition without consent, Mr Ferguson.'

'I have Judge Curran's consent.' Ferguson lifted the telephone from the front of the desk and placed it in front of Brown. Brown looked at it. That's how you got people to do things. You rearranged their world a little. It kept them off balance. You eased your way into their thoughts so that your face drifted unbidden into their mind at off moments.

'I knew Mrs Curran before her daughter's murder. She was always highly strung.'

'Her grasp on reality is tenuous.'

'Would you say she's capable of harm?'

'Are you? Which one of us isn't?'

'You know what I'm talking about?'

'You're asking me if Doris Curran could have killed her own daughter. Is that what you're asking me?'

Ferguson did not speak. The superintendent got to his feet.

He walked over to the bookcase and ran his index finger along the book spines.

'There are case histories of everything you can imagine in here. Parents killing children. Children killing parents. Paranoid schizophrenics who imagine that they are killing the devil.'

'So she could have done it?'

'It strikes me that you are in a better position to answer that than I am. You were there that night. You knew each member of the family. You are Judge Curran's man, are you not?'

'Everybody is somebody's man in this town, superintendent. There was a report. When she was admitted.'

'Yes.'

'I want to see it.'

'If you wish. Judge Curran has already read it.'

Doris was glad to see Ferguson coming but she is glad to see him go as well. His wife's name is Esther, like the Bible although Ferguson's Esther is not like Esther from the Bible, more like a harlot. He wants to know what happened. He wants to know what happened to Patricia. Everyone wants to know what became of her.

A friend of Desmond's, Iain Hay Gordon, was convicted and found insane though Doris found it hard to believe that skinny little man could murder anybody. She read the papers at the time. The prosecution said that Gordon kissed Patricia at the bottom of the driveway and then things got out of hand. He said that Gordon tried to touch her but she said, 'Don't, you beast,' and things got out of hand and that he lost control of his manly appetites.

Doris knew that Patricia would not put her lips to a man

such as Gordon. She would be as like to kiss a stick as kiss a bag of bones such as Gordon was. She knew the kind of men that her daughter liked, men smelling of cologne with a smile always on their lips and a lewd word.

When Patricia was small she would sit at the dressing table watching Doris put on her make-up and well she learned. Her father would watch her with a look as though he conjured something pleasant from long ago if only he could remember what it was.

One day Patricia removed his judge's wig from its tin box. It was a horrid, tatty thing. Patricia walked into the dining room and said, 'Ladies and gentlemen of the jury, his honour Mr Justice Curran, I condemn you to death.' We all laughed. But her father did not laugh but brought her to the outhouse and whipped her.

Doris had always wanted Patricia to know how dangerous the world was. Patricia had never seen the faces at the Broadmoor windows. The procuresses. The hollow-cheeked magdalens. Doris could feel Patricia's eyes following her around the house. She wanted to tell her not to let her eyes follow people that way.

The first time Doris heard of Thomas Cutbush was when she read his file from his admission to Broadmoor. The file lay open on her father's desk and she read it.

Description of Thomas Cutbush admitted from Holloway Prison

Born: 29th June 1866

Age: 24 years

Height: 5 ft 9 1/2 inches

Weight: 9 stone 6 1/2 pounds

Hair: black

Whiskers: black (very short)

Eyes: dark blue (very sharp)

Complexion: dark

Build: slight

Features: thin

Marks: slight bruise on left knee. 1 tooth out in front of upper jaw

When later that evening she saw a man looking at her from a window in D wing she knew it was Cutbush. He didn't push his face up against the bars like the others did. He stayed back in the shadows. You had to imagine the short black whiskers. The eyes. They say he lived in the Minories, beside Whitechapel. That he followed women home. Doris had to walk under his window every day. He was always there, watching her. She could tell. How still he was at his window. Saucy Jack.

They told her that Cutbush had died in 1903 but she knew that people like Cutbush never died. They were always in the shadows, just out of reach. You could feel the eyes on you. Dark blue. Very sharp.

Some nights she lay awake and knew that Cutbush was also awake in his cell with his whiskers black and his eyes so blue, so sharp.

The female lunatics who were trusted worked in the vegetable gardens outside her father's office. Sometimes she walked through the gardens with him, and they would glance up at her, mute and incurious. Their eyes dark with knowledge of atrocity. When she was older she would accompany her father on his rounds.

'Life is not all frocks,' he said. He kept a model of the human brain on his desk and showed her the grey ridged thing, pointing out the lobes and hemispheres. His father had been a butcher and he kept a slaughterhouse in the prison grounds.

Father read the newspapers everyday. Doris heard him say to the medical officer that the Jack the Ripper killings had stopped when Cutbush had been arrested. Doris sat beneath Father's desk and heard every word. About women dead in London alleys. The female parts mutilated. Terror abroad in the Whitechapel fog, the wreathing vapours.

Doris was not squeamish about medical matters. Broadmoor was as much a hospital as a prison. Lucy had sought to shield her from the patients but her father thought it was good for her to visit patients in the infirmary. She was familiar with a range of symptoms, the palsies, the compulsive behaviours, the self-harming. Patients slashed at themselves, burned their bodies, attempted to sever their own genitalia. When she saw a patient whose arms were tied to the metal bed frame with bandages, the prison doctor described him as an onanist. It was not uncommon for patients to throw off their clothes.

Lucy told her about Cutbush outside the gin houses. In the alleys around the Minories women dropped their inside clothes to fornicate with men, Lucy says. Doris did not know the meaning of the word fornication.

When Doris looked out of the window on a December evening to see a naked woman in the exercise yard she was not surprised. Frost had lain on the ground in the sunless yard since morning. The woman stood very still. She wore scapulars on string around her neck. Before she was taken by the arm and led away, Doris saw that her lips were moving, praying, reciting the names of God. Nude, enraptured.

PRELIMINARY ADMISSION REPORT 25TH NOVEMBER 1952

Mrs Doris Curran

Mrs Curran was admitted on 20th November 1952 on the advice of the family general practitioner, Dr Kenneth Wilson. She was in a withdrawn state, uncommunicative, and refusing food. It was assumed that her condition was a reaction to the sudden death of her nineteen-year-old daughter eight days previous, her delicate state of mind being adversely affected by the tragic events. She was kept under close observation for the first weeks of her hospitalisation although not thought a suicide risk. Visits from family were accompanied by extreme agitation such that she had to be sedated following the visit of her husband on 20th March.

Mrs Curran had been seen as a day patient on occasions in 1950 and 1951 after concerns had been raised by her husband and by the family doctor. She seems to have become fixated on her daughter Patricia's behaviour, which she regarded as errant in the extreme. She spoke often of Patricia's 'defiance' and suggested that there might be an element of sexual impropriety associated with Patricia's behaviour.

Patricia Curran, then aged seventeen, was seen in this office on 14th January 1951. She presented as a spirited, intelligent female. Some aspects of her demeanour were inappropriate to her age and station. She was given to some vulgarity in language. She admitted to smoking and to truancy from school on occasions. Her relations with males of her own age were of particular interest. She described them as 'callow' and 'only after one thing'. When her response was queried she said that she 'preferred a more mature man'. There was a degree of levity associated with her remarks, nonetheless they showed a precocious sexuality.

Patricia had attended a 'life class' at the College of Art. Her mother had found drawings made during the class under her bed and had brought them to the clinic without her daughter's knowledge. Mrs Curran thought that the drawings of the naked female form exhibited delinquency on the part of her daughter, if not deviancy, and asked if Patricia might be medicated. Medication was not considered appropriate.

When confronted with the drawings Patricia stated that her mother had 'no right' to remove them from her room. She refused to answer questions as to the appropriateness of the images. Aggressive tendencies were displayed during this interview.

On the whole Mrs Curran's concerns were considered valid. The Attorney General attended the clinic to hear the conclusions drawn following interviews with his daughter. As is to be expected, he had many questions on the subject of his daughter's mental health and queried the terms hyperesthesia and erotomania which were contained in the report. He expressed his reluctance to pursue the proposed course of medication for his daughter, instead suggesting that she be monitored by the family doctor, although he did express concern about Patricia's sometimes 'erratic' behaviour.

Subsequent to Patricia's murder, her medical files were requested by Chief Inspector Capstick of Scotland Yard, who had been assigned to the case at a late stage. Capstick's approach to the medical records was irregular. He did not seek a court order. He came to Holywell on 20th November and was shown to my office. In my absence he demanded to see the files there and then. He was told that the files were not to be released unless by court order, and certainly not without the permission of the Curran family. However Chief Inspector Capstick prevailed upon a junior staff nurse to fetch the files and when I arrived he had apparently read them. He seemed to think that the files confirmed public apprehensions that Patricia was a 'nympho' and wished me to confirm that she had 'got in a scrape' with 'one of her chaps on the way home'. I replied that the files were confidential medical records of a limited series of interviews and could not be regarded as clinically complete in any sense. Chief Inspector Capstick replied that he had got what he had wanted at any rate and left.

There was no further application for the files to be produced in court. It was suggested to me on several occasions that the legal parties were sensitive to the feelings of the Curran family and that the material contained in the files would be damaging to Patricia's character. I was made aware that the defence solicitor for Iain Hay Gordon, the man subsequently convicted for Patricia's murder, might approach me to testify as to her character but no such approaches were received.

Mrs Curran remained in a delicate condition. There were several episodes of psychosis and catatonia which were treated with tranquillisers although these sometimes had no discernible effect. Mrs Curran was given to excessive and purposeless motor activity. On occasions she walked from one end of her room to the other for periods of six hours. She gave no indication however that she was aware of the search for her daughter's killer or of the trial of Iain Hay Gordon for Patricia's murder. She did not mention her daughter's name during this period, although she sometimes mentioned her son Desmond with pride. Her husband came to see her once a week. She appeared withdrawn following these visits.

Mrs Curran was placed under continuous observation during the trial of Iain Hay Gordon. She mixed freely in the day room between the hours of nine and six and it was thought that some of the other patients might relate details of her daughter's death to her.

While observing Mrs Curran alone in her room after she had retired, the ward sister reported that the patient appeared to be hearing voices. I observed Mrs Curran and confirmed the sister's report. Mrs Curran appeared to be experiencing classic auditory hallucination. Judging by the tone of her responses the voices were by turn derogatory, commanding or preoccupying. Following several periods of observation I concluded that there were at least two principal voices. The primary voice preoccupied Mrs Curran to a large degree and she seemed to be able to converse easily, in a 'chatty' fashion, although she did seem to be struck silent on occasion.

The second voice provoked a more extreme reaction. Mrs Curran's responses were brief and it was evident that the voice spoke with some authority. She exhibited signs of stress and fear and remained unnaturally still when listening. Following exposure to this voice she resumed compulsive activities, hand-washing, pacing, etc.

An important outcome of Mrs Curran's treatment will be the elimination of these voices. The patient must be made aware of the fact that these voices are imaginary, a function of the unbalanced mind, and should not be indulged or negotiated with.

I remained unconvinced that the death of her daughter was the root cause of her psychosis since she had shown signs of difficulty before that date. Over the course of several interviews her upbringing and early childhood was investigated. It is a commonplace of analysis that the root cause of much psychosis lies in early childhood, but it may be thought that an upbringing in an institution such as Broadmoor might provide fertile ground for enquiry.

Seven

25TH JULY 1949

The trial of Robert Taylor for the murder of Mary McGowan opened at the law courts on Chichester Street on the 25th of July 1949. Mr Justice Shiel presided. It was a hot day and the courthouse and its environs assumed the aspect of some southern assize. The men dressed in black stood in rows to either side of the courthouse and their shadows were elongated on the pavement as though a noontime of consequence were on them. The women fell silent as Taylor's father and sister Madeleine alighted from a taxi. They stood to either side of the car door and waited for the last of their party to emerge. Some of the throng were neighbours and would have known Robert Taylor's fiancée of several weeks, Lily Jones, but they did not at first recognise her as she stepped from the car. Lily wore a long black dress, a black hat and a black mourning veil which concealed her face.

Lunn had suggested the widow's clothing, his strategy to draw the jury's sympathy from Mary McGowan's daughter, Kathleen, who would be in court to give evidence against her mother's killer. There were gasps from the crowd when Lily emerged from the car. They were reminded that this was a matter of blood and legacy. A young solicitor's apprentice, Paschal O'Hare, was in the crowd. A woman spoke to him as Lily mounted the courthouse steps: 'Good Fenian crop planted in the soil.' O'Hare took this as a reference to Mary McGowan.

People could see the shape of Lily's pregnancy through the black fabric. The trial would bring down judgement and retribution on the woman and her unborn child. She seemed a sorrowing figure, and the people jostled about her and more women and children joined the throng as though the town's barrios had emptied and marched upon the courthouse. Two dozen armed constabulary came around the corner of the building and stood in rank across the front of the courthouse. Lunn emerged from a black town car and took Lily's arm, escorting her to the top of the staircase. In the limestone portico he turned her towards the crowd and showed her to them as though she would enact for them a drama of family and vengeance. The crowd surged silently forward and the constables pushed them back with their rifle butts. Lunn led Lily into the courthouse.

Ferguson drove Curran to the courthouse in the Lancia. A police car led them through the crowd. Faces bent to stare through the window at Curran but he sat without moving and the populace stepped back from the car as though it was a cortège which made its way into the court precincts. Curran looked up once as Lunn made display of Lily at the top of the steps.

Curran wore a carnation in the buttonhole of his frock coat, a white winged collar and barrister's starched neckpiece. The crowd pressed after them and the porters pushed them back and closed and locked the iron gates.

All through the trial the sun beat down and it seemed that people did not know themselves or their city. The centre felt dusty, provincial, heatstruck. Aspects of the city that had remained unseen became apparent. Colonial architectures, cupolas, the city heat-hazed, lost in an oriental dream of itself. The harsh and atonal cries of newsvendors sound like calls to prayer, the sung-out stanzas of prophecy. Trains are put on, weekend specials, to carry trippers to the resort towns of Portrush and Bangor. They walk the promenades and tiled lidos, sundazed, lost. Illumination from strings of coloured lights falls across the esplanades at night and in the dimlit wind shelters and bandstands couples lie on the wooden benches or are driven by the night heat to stand against walls and trees like lewd statuary.

Patricia took the bus to Central station and walked to Crumlin Road. The porters and RUC men at the court buildings knew her. They'd let her in through back doors, lead her down corridors, passing the rooms where prison warders and guards drank tea, their boots unlaced, caps pushed back on their heads. Places where you heard the gaolhouse sounds, clankings and men cursing in the distance.

A warder called McConkey said he would bring her to the public gallery. He said that there was plenty of time and that he would show her the gallows. He led her through the damp limestone tunnel between the gaol and the courthouse. The dismantled scaffold was kept in the room below the execution chamber. McConkey kept trying to edge her up against the wall, the stacked members. He showed her where the main beam of the gallows fitted into the platform. He allowed her to work the trapdoor lever. A utilitarian clang in the shadowed spaces.

'You need to stand witness to an execution,' McConkey said, 'you never seen anything like it. A man dangling from the end of a rope. I was there on the solemn occasion they done Williams. Quick and clean, a textbook example, Mr Pierrepoint says to me afterwards. The condemned man was pronounced devoid of life forty minutes after for he has to dangle that long before the doctor is allowed near him.'

'Does it hurt?'

'Not a bit. The knot snaps the vertebrae. The spinal cord is severed. He hangs there. You can see the evidence of his excitement.'

Patricia didn't really know what he was talking about. She told Hilary what he had said afterwards.

'Did he really say that, Patricia?'

'Yes. He was red in the face when he said it.'

'I'm not surprised he was puffing and panting. A hanged man gets a stiffy when he dies. It's something to do with the blood pressure.'

'A stiffy?'

'A great big bloody horn from what they say.'

McConkey brought her to the condemned man's cell, the door to the gallows hidden behind a bookcase. McConkey said that Williams was the last man to occupy the cell. Nineteen years old. McConkey told Patricia about the moment when they pulled the bookcase back to reveal the doorway behind. Williams shook his head and smiled at the way he'd been fooled, a weary end-of-days smile, his hands tied together behind his back.

'Can they hang Taylor if he's found guilty?' Patricia said.

'He should be,' McConkey said, 'and in law there's no reason why he shouldn't.'

The space in the small burial yard at Crumlin Road that had been reserved for Taylor was in fact filled by Robert McGladdery after Lance Curran had convicted him and sentenced him to death for the murder of Pearl Gamble.

'The corpse of the deceased is left to hang for forty minutes,' McConkey said, 'then the doctor steps forward and pronounces life extinct. The corpse is cut down and brought for post-mortem.'

The warder opened the small ironbound door to the post-mortem room. There was a plain wooden table in the centre of the room with sluices leading to an open drain in the floor. A small trolley held scalpels and bone saws on its top deck and glass Kilner jars on the second tier. There was another door in the far wall.

'What's that for?'

'For interment of the deceased,' McConkey said. He took an iron key from the cluster at his belt and opened the brassbound lock. The door opened into a small high-walled yard. A gravelled sunless place with seven narrow graves without markers against the far wall.

'If Taylor is found guilty and hanged then he'll be buried right here.' McConkey stood beside the last grave. 'Beside our old pal Mr Williams.'

'I wouldn't like to be buried here.' Patricia shivering as she spoke.

'I wouldn't take a pension to be planted here either, miss, but it's not likely to happen to either of us. But we'll keep an eye on Mr Taylor for I believe a spot in this yard will be pegged out for him.'

'Those poor men,' Patricia said, 'not even a flower laid for them.'

'Murderers, the whole lot of them,' McConkey said. 'They

got their just deserts and good riddance.'

Patricia stared at the graves. It was the picture that would come into McConkey's mind when he heard about her murder. The girl with the downturned mouth standing alone in that unhallowed place.

McConkey showed her into a seat beside Harry Ferguson. The foreman of the jury kept looking towards Ferguson. Patricia remembered the feel of his overcoat against her cheek. The way he smelt of cologne and cigarette smoke. She noticed the way people nodded at him. Court clerks, policemen. The way they leaned over and whispered to him, bringing him stories, scandal, the information flow of the city, its spoken bounty.

More papers were brought to the judge by the clerk. Then the judge spoke to her father.

The courtroom was not as Patricia had imagined it might be. She had expected dread, a monstrous tribunal. Men gesturing and eloquent. But this room was quiet. One of the jury members looked as if he was asleep. Documents were being passed up to the judge. Her father sat at a wooden table, his head bent over an affidavit. There were dust motes in the air. It reminded her of schooldays, a classroom at Methody, late afternoon, a teacher's voice droning on.

As the day went on she started to see it differently. There were other things going on here, low-key and elaborate. The fabric of the courtroom gathered meaning to itself, the chipped benches and scuffed planks. Law reports stacked on the desk in front of the court clerk, books of lore and covenant. She saw George Hanna, the defence counsel. He was a sleek, plausible-looking man. Hanna paused behind her father and spoke but

Lance did not look up from the brief on the table in front of him.

Patricia thought that Taylor did not look old enough to die by hanging. She told Hilary that his attention wasn't on proceedings most of the time. He smiled at the public gallery or waved. And sometimes he would find something, a loose thread or a button on his jacket, and would examine it for hours, turning it this way and that as though he would learn the properties of it.

'Does he look wicked and depraved,' Hilary said, 'an evil monster?'

'He looks like somebody's little brother,' Patricia said.

'A babyface killer,' Hilary said. 'No one suspects him.'

'You could see him delivering things. Newspapers,' Patricia said.

'He finds his way into his victims' confidence. Before they know it they are ensnared in his web of intrigue. They plead for mercy but though his eyes are smiling his heart is made of stone.'

'He's a fidget. Jumps about the place.'

'Probably the remorse. Gnawing at him. What's the gen on the courtroom? I'd say you could cut the tension with a knife. A man on trial for his very life. What was your father like?' Hilary said. 'Was he heroic? Standing up for truth? Stern but just?'

Lance seemed to be addressing himself to an office superior to others in the court. They left space around his desk. Solicitors entered it respectfully with documents, withdrew without speaking. A higher purpose was being explored. Patricia kept her head down so that he would not see her, but Lance did not look at the public gallery.

Every few minutes it seemed that Taylor remembered where he was and he would look around. His eyes kept going to the second row of the gallery. His father and mother sat there. His father looked like a shipyard worker. He was wearing a serge suit and he held a cloth cap between his hands. His eyes travelled over the members of the jury, looking each of them up and down, returning always to the foreman. A girl sat beside Taylor's father. She was wearing a black dress and veil as though she was in mourning. She moved uncomfortably in her seat, standing once as if she had cramp, and Patricia saw that she was pregnant. The girl had an engagement ring on her hand. She kept looking up at Taylor but he did not look back.

'Up the duff,' Hilary said later that evening. 'Mr Babyface isn't so innocent after all. At least he intends to make a decent woman of her. Was she pretty?'

'From what you could see,' Patricia said. The girl kept her head down when she wasn't looking up at Taylor. Her veil covered her face but Patricia could see her eyes behind the fringe, moving ceaselessly about the courtroom.

'I think she hates all of us,' Patricia said. She did not understand why Lily had chosen to wear a veil. She stayed that way through the whole trial although it was warm in the courtroom and the girl must have felt the heat.

'Bloody cheek,' Hilary said, 'a shopgirl or the like. Who does she think she is, Mata bloody Hari?'

'Mr Curran, are you ready to call your first witness?' Curran got to his feet. He waited until the courtroom fell silent before he spoke. He carried a mute authority and Patricia could see how the jury and the public gallery turned to him as though he was in fact the judge.

Kathleen McGowan wore a black linen suit and a white cotton blouse with a plain collar. Her hair was pinned close to her head. She did not look at Robert or Lily as she walked to the dock. She wore no make-up. She looked plain-spoken, Quakerish. She passed in front of Harry Ferguson in the front row of the public gallery and he smelt coal-tar soap. Ferguson knew what Curran was about to do, Kathleen looking like some Protestant martyr closing in on God.

The solicitor Lunn leaned back in his chair so that he was close to Ferguson and spoke softly.

'Curran's going to strip his own witness to the bone. If I were you I'd find another line of work, Harry. Or another boss.'

Kathleen McGowan took the oath and stood in the witness box facing the bench. Robert Taylor sat in the dock behind her.

'Do you recognise the accused?' Curran said. Kathleen looked back over her shoulder.

'Yes, that is Robert the Painter.'

'Did he work for your mother?'

'He came round with Mr Barrett of Sunnyside Street. They painted the house.'

'The house in Newington?'

'Yes.'

'How many times?'

'I beg your pardon?'

'How many times did you see Taylor working at your mother's house?'

'I remember four times.'

Curran motioned to a uniformed policeman who stepped forward with a heavy spanner. He placed the labelled spanner on the bench in front of the judge.

'An American-gauge seven-eighths spanner,' Curran said. 'Is there such a spanner in your house?'

'I have never seen one.'

The policeman stepped forward again and placed a carving knife on the bench. The blade of the knife was bent, the steel grotesquely kinked halfway between the handle and the tip.

'Do you recognise this knife?'

'It is our knife,' Kathleen said.

'Our knife?'

'From our kitchen. I saw my mother use it to cut bread that morning.'

'Was it bent then?'

'No, it wasn't.'

Curran nodded to the constable, who stepped forward bearing a cotton frock. The frock was stiff in his arms. There was a dark slurry of blood and dried stock in its folds and pleats. The front and bodice of the dress was rent with knifemarks. Sun fell upon the dress from the high windows, giving the material the appearance of some gorgeous apparel of deep red velvet, a brocaded princess of the dead presented to some dread ball.

'Is this your mother's dress?'

'Yes.'

'The one she was wearing on the morning of the murder?'

'It is. We bought it. We went together to the city centre.'

The girl's voice was steady and her back was straight. The judge nodded approval at her demeanour. There would be no outbursts in his courtroom. Patricia's face was white and she was staring at her father. Ferguson could hear the tremor in the girl's voice, the deep, harming undertone. Kathleen McGowan was in shock. Ferguson had seen it in servicemen. Men sitting alone in scenes of recent carnage, their eyes empty. They answered to the medics without looking at them. They spoke softly for they spoke with the voices of the dead.

'The photographs,' Curran said. The policeman brought forward a cardboard folder with the coroner's crest on the cover. The tipstaff opened the folder and removed a sheaf of monochrome prints. Curran caused them to be shown to the jury and then displayed to the witness. Kathleen McGowan grasped the rail in front of her.

'Is this your mother?' Curran asked. Kathleen nodded then said, 'Yes,' quietly, though it would have been also true for her to say no, Ferguson thought, for how could the profane creature in the autopsy photographs be her mother?

'Is this your mother?' Curran held up another photograph and Kathleen assented.

'What's he doing?' Patricia whispered in Ferguson's ear.

'He's making sure that the jury get to see her mother's injuries.'

'It's terrible.'

Curran showed Kathleen the prints one by one then put the last photograph on the bench and sat down. He took an affidavit from the desk in front of him and began to read.

'Are you finished with the witness, Mr Curran?' the judge asked.

'I am, your honour.' Kathleen McGowan started to get down from the box but Hanna rose to his feet.

'A few questions if you don't mind, Miss McGowan.'

'You may sit if you wish, Miss McGowan,' the judge said.

'No thank you.'

The autopsy photographs had been left on the evidence

bench, in the late morning heat. The paper exuding the scent of developing fluid. From the gallery Ferguson could just see the shape of the woman's body, the nude form against the monochrome, lost in the deep shadow. He could feel Patricia's thigh against his as Hanna cross-examined Kathleen, his manner warm, asking her if it was true that her mother was 'a generous large-hearted type of woman and a good devout practising Catholic'.

Kathleen stumbled as she stepped down from the witness box and Hanna stepped forward to steady her as the judge called the lunch recess.

Outside Ferguson stood in the shade of the portico and lit a cigarette. He held the lit cigarette cupped and hidden in his hand, furtive doings his stock in trade. He felt Patricia take him by the arm.

'Why is Father being so cruel to that girl?' she said.

'I'm not sure if he sees her,' Ferguson said. 'I think he only sees his case.'

'I shall tell him what I think,' Patricia said. 'Can I have a pull of your fag?'

'Not here, Patricia.'

'Will she ever get over what happened to her mother?' Patricia said.

'She'll get over it,' Ferguson said. 'People do.'

'But she'll never get over Father, that's what you're thinking, isn't it? I could see it in her eyes. He might as well have been hitting her with that bloody spanner.'

'The case is there to be won.'

'The way he's going at it, you'd think he had a bet on it to win.'

'What did you say?'

'I know he gambles, Harry. All my friends talk about it. They hear their parents talk about it. You know the way parents whisper in corners and think nobody hears?'

Ferguson did know about people thinking themselves unheard to the world.

'You don't say very much, Harry.'

'No?'

'I know why.'

'I'm all ears.'

'Silence makes people uncomfortable. They start talking to fill up the quiet. Next thing they're telling you their life story.'

'You're very sharp, Patricia. Tell me something. What did you think of Hanna's cross-examination?'

'He was kinder than Father.'

'Was he?'

'What are you trying to say?'

'All this decent, kind-hearted woman nonsense? What was he really trying to do?'

'I don't know.'

'Making sure the jury knew she was a Catholic. Driving the point home. He wasn't trying to make them sympathise. The opposite. He was reminding them that she was a Fenian.'

'There's a meanness about people in this town,' Patricia said.

*

The trial resumed after lunch with legal argument concerning the admissibility of the dead woman's identification evidence.

Hanna argued badly. He removed his wig several times to wipe sweat from his forehead. He said that Mary McGowan did not think that she was dying. She had not asked for her husband. She had not asked for the last rites. Her thoughts were of a 'terrestrial' nature. Therefore her dying testimony, according to the law, was inadmissible.

'If she was a good woman like Mr Hanna said before,' Patricia said, 'then she wouldn't name an innocent man.'

'That's right,' Ferguson said, 'you're learning. Hanna's out of his depth. Making a bad case worse. If you've nothing to say, then best say nothing.'

Curran was clipped and precise. Mary McGowan had told several witnesses that she was dying. She spoke calmly and without drama to her neighbour, Mrs Rafferty, mother of the twins, to neighbour Robert Skillen and to Detective Sergeant Davis who had sat at her bedside in hospital that night. The judge ruled that testimony to the victim's dying statements was admissible. Mrs Rafferty went into the witness box. Curran guided her through the events of the murder. She was followed by DS Davis, who confirmed that Mary McGowan had named Taylor as her attacker. Curran had taken command of the courtroom. Ferguson thought he was like a figure of the testament from his youth. *The voice he spoke with was that of the Lord and he was wroth.* Patricia told Hilary afterwards that she felt as if she had found herself in some theatre of old where a tale of blood and guile was enacted. Lily sat unmoved beneath her veil. Taylor in the dock between two warders, the music-hall imp, the child actor ready to move centre stage, freckle-faced and manic.

*

When Patricia arrived home the housekeeper, Mrs McCrink, was waiting for her in the hallway.

'I thought you'd never come home, Patricia.'

'What's up, Agnes?'

'Your mother.'

'She got the heebie-jeebies again?'

'I had to call Dr Wilson. He gave her a sedative, but I was afraid to leave her alone.'

'Where's the sainted Desmond?'

'Master Desmond must be at the law library.'

'Surprised he wasn't in court to see Father tormenting that poor girl.'

'Please, Patricia, will you go up to her?'

'Of course I will. Though much good may it do. You know what she's like with me when she has a turn.'

'You could brush her hair. That calms her down.'

'Yes, you're right.'

'Mr Curran will probably dine at his club.'

'If he's any sense he'll steer clear of here.'

'You will go up, won't you, Patricia?'

'Don't worry, Aggie dear, I'll brush the head off her if it helps. Just wait until I get changed.'

Doris sat alone in her room. Dr Wilson had waited to see her take the tablets he had brought for her, but she only pretended to swallow them, hiding them the way Lucy had shown her at Broadmoor.

Through the bedroom window she had watched Patricia walking towards the house from the bus stop. She saw her stop on the driveway and lift up her school jumper. She worked at the waistband of her skirt then let the jumper fall back again. At the start of that term Doris had noticed how short Patricia's skirt was. She put her hand on Patricia's waist and it was just as she thought. Her daughter had rolled the waistband of the skirt to bring the hem above her knee. They had words about it. Patricia was not a mill girl and Doris told her so and had forbidden her to go to the pictures with the Douglas girl who was as common as they come for all her father was clergy. Your winsome air does not fool me, miss, Doris would think with her mouth in a grim set, nor does your horsey face. Doris knew what went on in a stable block.

The year after they were married Ferguson had taken Lance and Doris to a stables near Newtownards. Ferguson wanted Lance to join a syndicate to buy a racehorse. The stables owner had taken them to see a mare covered by a stallion. Ferguson had suggested that Doris might like to take tea with the owner's wife but Lance said no, what is it but nature? And Doris was not shocked, how could she be, with all that she had seen at Broadmoor and how the stallion did in daylight what others strained at in the darkness.

Down below in the shrubbery she saw Patricia settle her skirt and take a small mirror and a handkerchief from her school bag. She wet the corner of the handkerchief and rubbed at the lipstick, then at her eye make-up, checking in the mirror to see if it was gone. The sneaky gestures, one after the other, her daughter thinking herself hidden in the shrubbery. Doris keeping her under surveillance. Doris the watcher from the window.

Eyes dark blue. Very sharp.

Doris had faced Patricia with the evidence of her disobedience over the years. A list that was forever to hand when she needed to speak to Patricia. Bazooka bubblegum. Lipsticks. Cigarettes. Mademoiselle magazine with advice on 'how to steal a man's heart'. Valentine cards. A letter from a lovesick boy. All Patricia's smutty schoolgirl doings which went along with the hitched-up skirt and the caked-on make-up to say only one thing to a mother's worried mind.

There was no doubt in Doris's mind that there was talk about Patricia. The other mothers heard it from their daughters. That her classmates considered Patricia *fast*.

When Doris was ten years old she had watched the line of washhouse girls walk through the icy yards to their work in the prison laundry. She asked Lucy who they were. Them is the trollops, Lucy said, who made their bed and now are in a requirement to lie on it. The girls looked pale and underfed in darned pinafores. Their ankles were bare to the frost. You thought of the industrial poor. Of slum folk. One of them turned as she drew level with Lucy. The girl spat at her feet.

'Keep tha beaky face to thaselve.' Her face was pale and vehement. She looked down at Doris.

'Who would set a loon like thee to mind a child?' The girl had a hoarse, mannish voice and black eyes.

'Get away from us,' Lucy said.

'What landed thee in this place?' the girl said. 'You've the look of one who's done time on her back. They do say them that have slain their own bairns are sent here.'

Doris felt Lucy's hand tighten on hers so that she cried out.

The noise drew the attention of a female warder. The turnkey called out to the girl to get back in line. The girl smiled at Doris. Doris expected some gap-toothed slum grin but the girl's teeth were white and perfect like those of a film star.

'Keep tha head high and tha knees closed, girlie, and you'll not end up like me and her.'

The girl joined the line again. The laundry workers filed through the top gate, shuffling, tainted.

Doris turned away from the window when she heard Patricia's tread on the stairs. She knew that Mrs McCrink would send her up to brush her hair and calm her down before Lance got home. Doris wasn't born yesterday. She knew how to put a stop to their gallop. She saw the door handle turn slowly. Patricia trying to gain entry to the only room where Doris knew any peace. But Doris had locked the door the minute Mrs McCrink had left, knowing she would be in cahoots with Patricia. The door handle turned slowly again. It was like a film with a lady in a bedroom and evil without measure on the other side of the door, the night-prowled hallway. It was almost dark outside now and sleet blew against the bedroom window. The coming night was all about her and she was afraid.

At Broadmoor there had been a siren to warn the countryside that an inmate had escaped. The hospital and its inmates were in the consciousness of the communities surrounding the asylum, a deep tainted undertow. Madmen abroad on the moors. Child-killers at large in the byways. The local people knew the felonious roll call. William Chester Minor. Kelly. Dadd. They were familiar with their crimes, their dark proclivities, their unsated lusts. The siren was sounded on the night of 10th September 1923.

Townspeople sat up in bed, ran to their children's rooms, their worst fears confirmed. The sound rolled out from the front tower of Broadmoor, the dire tocsin sounding in the night. In Bagshot. In Owlsmoor. The siren rang twice for two minutes then ceased. There was the baying of hounds from the direction of the prison.

'Mother?' The voice sounded like that of Patricia but she could not be certain. The mad were cunning and had many ruses. Doris thought she would stay quiet. She would not say a word.

'Mother, it's Patricia. You can unlock the door. I thought we could have a chat and I could brush your hair.' The doorknob rattled again. The demented were persistent. You never saw the face until the end, the killer's face. White, harried, intent. Reaching for you with his long strangling fingers. Raising above you the long sharp knife.

Doris got up and went to the wardrobe. She took her dressmaking box from the wardrobe floor. The dressmaking box had a padded lid with a floral pattern. It had belonged to her mother and Doris had not been allowed to play with it. There were spools of bright thread and needles which glittered. The box had the feel of something from an old tale of malice, of fingers pricked on spindles, the needles glittering, stepmothers hollow with envy.

Patricia knocked on the door and rattled the brass doorknob. Outside the wind howled and the bare trees rattled. Doris lifted the top tray out of the knitting basket and took the dressmaking scissors from underneath.

'Please, Mother.'

There was an opening in the dressing table between the top

surface and the drawers where Doris kept cotton wool. She slipped the shears into the opening and arranged cotton wool around them. Then she went to the door and opened it.

'Honestly, Mother,' Patricia said, 'you shouldn't lock the door. What if there was an emergency or something?'

Patricia had taken off her school uniform and was wearing her Chinese silk robe. She had tied her hair back from her face, walking barefoot around the room. She straightened the bedspread. She took shoes from the floor and placed them on the shoe rack. A dress was laid over the back of a chair. Patricia lifted it and put it on a hanger in the wardrobe. Deft and homely gestures. Folding and arranging. The world put to rights in small ways. Patricia talking about her mother's day, ornamenting it with small talk and generalities.

Doris wasn't falling for any of it. Doris had her hand on the handle of the shears under the dressing table. She could hear bare feet padding about the room behind her. It made the hair on the back of her neck stand up. Stealing up behind you. The stealthy barefoot tread. *All the girls liked a lark with Thomas Cutbush. All the girls liked Tom.*

'Would you like me to do your hair now, Mother?' Patricia said. *Don't touch the locks now, girls. You know Thomas doesn't like the locks touched.* Doris withdrawing the shears from the opening. Knowing there would only be one chance. She could hear the rustle of the silk gown. Headlights swept across the room from the window in front of the dressing table. Doris looked out of the window and saw the Lancia pull into the driveway. The rear door opened and Lance got out. Lance looked up at the bedroom window. Doris shrank back.

Thomas stepped back into the shadow. Tom knows the law

when he sees it. There would be another chance to put manners on the saucy bitch.

The dressmaker's shears fell from Doris's hand. Patricia heard them strike the floor. She picked them up.

'Silly. You could have stabbed yourself in the foot. Was that Father's car?'

'Yes. Go to bed, Patricia.'

'Not on your nelly, Doris Curran, I've your hair to do.'

'Do as you are bid, Patricia. Your father will be coming to bed. He has court tomorrow and will be tired. And he may notice the smell of cigarette smoke from you, do you want to take that chance? You may fool him by removing your uniform before coming to my room, but you will not fool me.'

Patricia tucked the hairbrush under her arm. She gathered her mother's hair with both hands and twisted it away from her neck.

'You have such silky hair. Mine's like a wire brush.'

Patricia reached under her arm for the brush, still holding her mother's hair with her left hand. The things that pass between women. Tasks set. Identifying small needs in each other and attending to them. Tending and flattering. That was what Doris had tried to teach Patricia over the years. There was only a certain amount of love in the world. You had to be frugal with it. It had to be eked out over a lifetime. Not squandered. Not wasted in longing glances at men old enough to be your father.

As Patricia raised the brush Doris took it from her and threw it into the corner of the room. Patricia flushed.

'That's a silly thing to do, Mother.'

'You have no right to speak to your mother like that.'

The raised voices heard downstairs. Lance Curran standing at the front window, his hands clasped behind his back, staring into the dark. He heard Patricia's bedroom door slam. He would wait downstairs until Doris had gone to bed.

Eight

The public gallery was full for the second day of Taylor's trial. The crowd outside the courthouse had grown. Ferguson found himself looking around for Patricia but he could not see her. People were jostling each other at the front of the queue. Ferguson walked past the uniformed policeman at the front door and found a seat. Lily sat at the front of the gallery, still wearing her widow's clothing. Patricia sat down beside him. He felt her weight against his, smelt her perfume. She was sixteen, his master's daughter. She turned her dark eyes on him.

'God it's hot in here,' she said. He could see fine beads of perspiration on her upper lip. He wondered if she felt it, the stirrings, the deep, transgressive undertow.

The morning was given over to medical evidence. The pathologist, Dr J. A. Johnston, detailed the victim's injuries. Multiple incised wounds. Bleeding from mouth and both ears. *Die, bitch.* Swollen, fractured, burned. An air of ordeal about what had happened to Mary McGowan. She had been subject to medieval practices, torments of the flesh. Ferguson found himself thinking about pincers, implements of burning and rending, demands for repentance. Curran drawing out the evidence, letting it hang in the air. Hanna trying to suggest that McGowan was driven to hysteria by pain. That in her extremity and confusion she lashed out, naming an innocent man.

Taylor listened intently. His expression did not change, his

Bobby Breen look. He had nothing to do with these terrible events although Ferguson knew that Taylor was intrigued by what the pathologist was saying. He could see Taylor's right hand. He had grasped the material of his trousers between his finger and thumb and he was working it, balling and rubbing it. Testing the quality of the material. Ferguson thought of him bent over Mary McGowan, at work with knife and hammer, learning what the flesh would bear, apprentice to the arts of pain. The pincers. The rack.

Lily knew in her heart what Taylor had been up to with Mary McGowan. It was the way he was. The way he pinched her and fondled her. The way he wanted her to do things all the time. Things you couldn't tell anyone about. Asking her questions. Does that hurt? If I do it there does it feel the same? Lily going along with it. All his rubbings and smellings.

Lily liked being behind the veil. She felt like a lady with a mystery and secrets that none could know save she. The veiled lady. The spectators parted for her when she walked into the courtroom. Mr Hanna and Mr Lunn would open doors for her, pull out chairs for her to sit down. There were little gestures of gallantry. Not like the crown QC, Mr Curran. He'd sit very quiet at his desk until it was his turn, then he was all scorn and cutting words. Her sister-in-law Martha said that he was handsome and that he had been an officer in the army but Lily didn't think there was anything handsome about him. She didn't like the way his mouth turned down at the corners. It made her think of one of those cruel men in uniform you saw on the newsreels from the war.

During a prison visit Taylor had told Lily he'd seen Curran

at Dunmore Park at the dog racing one night. He said he'd seen him with the collar of his coat turned up, placing bets at the Tote hatch, but Lily didn't think that was true. Mark my words, Taylor said, I can spot a gambling man a mile off.

Taylor recognised another gambler in Lance Curran. All put to chance and all made forfeit. He recognised the demeanour. The hangdog mien. He saw what was unwholesome in the man. The betting slip in the hand, the face pinched with vice.

Kempton Park. Haydock. The names coming in off the wireless. Races that you would never see, the horses labouring towards the line, the fog of their breath.

'The type of man he is,' Taylor said, 'he couldn't see two flies running up a windowpane without making a bet in his head as to which one would breast the tape.'

Lily got a start when she looked along the front row of the public gallery and saw a girl who was the dead spit of Curran, with the same mouth turned down at the corners. She told Taylor on a visit that evening what she had seen, and Taylor had replied that he had seen her too and that it was Curran's daughter. He said she looked like a saucy one. She'd eat the face clean off you if you gave her half a chance. The girl was wearing a Methody school uniform, where all the nobby bitches went. The Methody girls had a reputation. Them girls spend as much time on their back as they do on their hind legs, Taylor said.

Taylor tried to say that one of the Methody girls had gone with him to Lady Dixon's park after dark and how she was dying for it. Lily said she didn't believe him, then wished she'd kept her big mouth shut. The rest of the visit was all spiteful remarks and comments about her appearance.

But Lily couldn't get the Curran girl out of her head. She

saw the way she watched her father. Like she was heart-scared of him but also that she would do his bidding to the last. She remembered wishing Curran ill-will. She remembered wishing that his daughter be taken away from him the way that Curran was trying to take Taylor away from her and see how he would feel about it then. If she thought about it hard enough she could make it happen. She was the veiled lady. She was the keeper of mystery.

Patricia told Ferguson that she had bunked off school for a second day. She looked as if she hadn't slept. There were dark shadows under her eyes. Ferguson hadn't slept either. He'd lain awake waiting for Esther to come in. Waited until he heard a car in the street, the key in the door and Esther coming up the stairs, carrying her shoes in her hand, entering the spare bedroom. When he was sure she was asleep he went downstairs. He picked up her wrap from the bannisters and smelt it, the perfume, the bar-room smells, loneliness. Her other life.

DI Thornton and DC Davis, who had been first to the murder scene, were called to the witness box. Davis said that he had been summoned to Ponsonby Avenue when John Caughey, a journalist and neighbour of the McGowans, entered the Antrim Road barracks. Caughey informed him that a lady had been attacked in Newington. Davis followed Caughey to the scene.

Davis said that they went to 18 Ponsonby Avenue, where he found the front door open. He entered the house. There was a bent and bloodstained knife on the table. There was a set of dentures and a large spanner on the floor. A bloodied earring lay beside the spanner. There was blood on the floor, on the walls and on the ceiling. Davis proceeded to number 19, the Rafferty house, where he found Mrs McGowan being held by Mrs Rafferty, Mrs McGowan a bloodstained marionette in her neighbour's arms.

Curran asked Davis if Mrs McGowan had spoken. He said that she had.

'What did she say?'

'Thank God the police have come. Please don't leave me. I am going to die.'

'Did you later try to ascertain her state of mind?'

'I asked her some time later if she thought she would recover.'

'What did the victim say in reply?'

'She said, "No, dear. I'm going to die. I know it."'

'What happened then?'

'I asked Mrs McGowan what had taken place. She said it was Robert, Robert the Painter. He works for Barrett. She said he asked to use the telephone, then he got her by the neck and started to choke her.'

The policeman said he went to the back of the garden of number 19 to write up his notebook. Davis then travelled to hospital with the victim and stayed by her bedside. At 7 p.m. she recovered consciousness. Davis asked her again what had happened. She said, 'It was Robert the Painter who worked for Barrett. I'm sure it was Robert. I knew him all right. It's all true.'

Ferguson shaking his head as Curran sat down.

'What is it?' Patricia said.

'You tell me.'

'That bit at the end. *I knew him all right. It's all true.*'

'Got it in one. Police-words added on.'

'Yes. It's not the kind of thing she would have said.'

'The bloody police. They can't help themselves. Anything else?'

Patricia frowned. 'Why would you ask somebody who was hurt if they thought they were going to recover? What sort of question is that?'

'Good. What else? Look for the unnecessary detail.'

'The notebook. Why did he mention writing up his notes?'

'Yes. He wouldn't have mentioned it if he had been writing up his notes the way he was supposed to. He's trying to cover himself. His nibs has noticed it too.' Ferguson nodded towards the defence QC, Hanna, who was getting to his feet.

'Is that bad?'

'No. Davis is an old hand. He won't admit anything to Hanna.'

Hanna suggested to Davis that he 'made his notes correspond with Mrs Rafferty's statements'. He asked Davis when had he in fact written up the notes. Davis replied that he had told the story 'as fairly and as straight and honestly as I could'. Hanna asked that Davis's notebook should be admitted as evidence.

DI Thornton followed Davis into the box. Thornton described his preliminary interview with Taylor. The police Humber arriving at his home, the long black car coming to rest in the empty street, the sun beating down on it, two policemen alighting carefully from it, grave in their belted tunics, entering the story carefully, knowing that they must uphold their place in the narrative.

Ferguson leaned across to Patricia.

'Let's see what Taylor was up to, the little weasel.'

From the start Taylor denied that he had anything to do with the assault, according to Thornton. Taylor had opened the door to the policemen and Thornton had noted five long scratches on Taylor's left cheek. The scratches were fresh and stood out against Taylor's fair complexion. Thornton noticed that his colleague Davis's eyes kept returning to Taylor's marked cheek. Thinking of the struggle that had taken place, the extremity which had driven a respectable lady like Mrs McGowan to such an act, the primal clawing.

The young man told Thornton he had walked into the city at 9.45 a.m. He had stopped at his newsagent's, the Daisy, and bought a paper. He went to visit his friend Billie Booth, who worked at the City Hall and who, he said, owed him £5. He wanted to use the £5 to pay for a taxi for his wedding. He did not see Booth. He then went to see Lily at her home in Lilliput Street at 12.30.

Thornton said they had then left the Taylor house and gone to Lilliput Street. Lily and her sister, Mary Erskine, confirmed that Taylor had been there. But the rest of it didn't stand up. The newsagent told Thornton that Taylor hadn't been there. He was adamant about it. Billie Booth said that he had never borrowed money off Taylor.

Lance Curran's tone was soft. He removed himself from the testimony. Thornton was a big man, burly, authoritative. When he removed his cap his hair was carefully combed. He had what was described as a Clark Gable moustache. A big man's vanities. A touch of burlesque about him, the carnival barker, pomaded and vain. Drawing in the audience, asking that the jury trust his account, to help them find a way through these shifting and allusive tales of the city.

Thornton, accompanied by a Sergeant Hughes, had returned to Taylor's house at 3 p.m. Taylor and Mary Erskine, Lily's sister, had continued with preparations for the wedding, persuading the wedding car firm to give them credit. As they were leaving the Williamson car office after signing sureties, they found Thornton and Hughes waiting for them. Taylor was taken to Glenravel Street barracks for further questioning.

Taylor was taken to an interrogation room. Curran asked Thornton to describe the room. There were no windows. There was a portrait of the king on the wall, which bore no other device. Taylor was seated at a plain table under a bare light. His interrogator faced him on the other side. The public recognised what was happening. It was how these things were meant to be conducted, the threads of the story being pulled together again, structure reasserting itself.

The jury followed Thornton's testimony closely. Despite the pathologist's careful scientific language, the medical evidence had shaken them. Not just the description of the victim's injuries but the sense it gave them of the attack, the unhinged moments. They needed Thornton to take control, big-boned, handsome. They imagined the portrait of the king, the melancholy regal features.

During Thornton's questioning Taylor once more denied he had been to Ponsonby Avenue that morning. Thornton said he had asked Taylor to remove his overcoat and jacket. The DI had examined both garments then removed them from the room. He had scraped dried blood from Taylor's instep into a sheet of white paper. 'Did you search the accused's garments?' Curran said.

'Yes.'

'Did you find a bill for twelve pounds nine shillings payable on that very day?'

'I did.'

'But you didn't find any money on the accused's person with which he might settle that bill.'

'No.'

'Did he admit he knew Mrs McGowan?'

'Cool as a cucumber. Said she always called him Robert as well.'

'What happened then?'

'I brought in his coat and his jacket and questioned him as to the presence of blood on them.'

'What did he reply?'

'He said it must be paint.'

'What did you do then?'

'I touched my finger to the stain and pressed my finger against the table so that he could see that it did not look like paint. That the substance on his coat was in fact blood.'

The bloodied fingermark was to remain on the scrubbed deal surface of the table during each of the subsequent interrogations. Taylor glanced at it every time he was brought into the room, as he was intended to, Thornton thinking that the admonitory finger would work on his mind, but the young man seemed immune to it.

'There were scratches on his face?' Curran said.

'Five big scrabs. He said his sister's youngster must have done it.'

Curran paused. Letting the image sink in. The young man sitting in the interrogation room, pale-faced, marked. Something primitive about the nail-marked face, the world of biting and tearing, wanting the jury to appreciate what Mary McGowan had become.

At that point the duty officer had entered the interrogation room and informed Thornton that Mrs Shiels from number 28 Ponsonby Avenue had made a statement saying that she had seen and recognised Taylor on the adjacent Atlantic Avenue a few minutes before Mary McGowan had been attacked.

'At that point I concluded the interview,' Thornton said.

'Had the defendant anything to add?'

'Not at that point. However I returned to his cell later that evening and told him he was to be charged with the murder of Mrs McGowan. I cautioned him that anything he might say at that point could be used in evidence.

'Did he make any reply?'

'He said, "Just say I'm innocent. That's all."'

Nine

Hanna and Lunn came to Taylor's cell directly from court. They took him through his testimony. Hanna said they'd had a stroke of luck. Taylor had the same blood group as Mary McGowan.

'Now we have to account for each bloodstain,' Lunn said, 'for Curran will crucify us if we don't get it right.'

The two men enacted various scenarios in which the blood from a nosebleed might have fallen on the areas of clothing discovered by the prosecution. They made Taylor lie on his back, sit with his elbows on his knees. Hanna intent on making a piece of theatre out of the testimony, Lunn more calculating, working out the angles, anticipating Curran's objections and challenges. Late in the evening the warder, McCullough, slid open the spy-hole and watched them for several minutes. Hanna blustering like some Elizabethan travelling player, master of animals and fools. Lunn brooding over his stagecraft, refining the stances which would allow blood to flow on to Taylor's overcoat, his socks and underpants, the instep of his shoe.

McCullough went back to his fellow warders where they sat in the central guardhouse.

'It's a regular bedlam in there, I can tell you that,' he said. He related what he had seen in the cell, the two impresarios and Taylor between them, shining with malice. McCullough was a religious man and he was uncomfortable with what he had seen, the staging of testimony by actors in some backstreet playhouse of the damned.

As he left the courthouse Ferguson's arm was held. One of the men he had seen sitting at McKenzie's bar, in a pinstripe jacket and docker's overalls.

'Mr McKenzie needs a word in the ear,' the man said.

'He's sequestered with the jury. He can't talk to me.'

'He's in the International Hotel. You'll find him at the tradesman's entrance, Amelia Street, at half eleven.'

'You tell McKenzie that if he's seen talking to me, the whole trial is blown out of the water.'

'Mr McKenzie knows that. Who's going to see you? And if anybody does they know to stay blind.'

Ferguson waited in the foyer of the Reform Club until eleven thirty. It was raining outside. A few vehicles passed outside. Last buses, a police tender. People hurrying past under umbrellas as though the city was subject to curfew. He looked for an umbrella from the porter but there was none so he turned up his collar and pulled the brim of his hat down over his face.

He met no one as he walked down Donegall Place and under the City Hall. He turned on to Howard Street and then on to Great Victoria Street. As he turned on to Amelia Street he saw Esther. She was standing under an umbrella outside the porter's lodge of the Europa. He crossed the street to her.

'What business do you have at this time of night in an alleyway like that?' she said. *The same business as you were conducting in that hotel perhaps*, he thought, but he did not say it.

'How are you getting home?' he said.

'I'm waiting for a taxi,' she said. She was wearing a dark dress and the umbrella was black so that she looked like a mourner, and he wondered how she would look at his own grave and whether she would become it.

'You could wait with me,' she said, 'we could go home together.'

'I can't,' he said, 'I have business with a man. But I'll be home later.' She inclined her head so that he could no longer see her face. He heard a taxi approaching.

'Perhaps you would hold the door for me?' she said as the car pulled alongside. Ferguson took the umbrella from her and held it over her head as she got into the car. This was the matter of their marriage, he thought. Gestures of hollow courtliness. Minor kindnesses, costing little.

Amelia Street had been known in the war as a place where women traded their bodies to servicemen and to naval workers. The prostitution had been tolerated until Wiley Harris stabbed Harry Coogan to death in a row over payment. Harris was hanged at Shepton Mallet and the police had halted the trade in the street. But it seemed to Ferguson that the women had not left the street, that there were lewd whisperings in the shadows.

He saw the glow of a cigarette under a shop awning, McKenzie's face lit from below as he cupped the cigarette and pulled on it. Ferguson nodded to him and stepped under the canvas awning.

'That's a great evening, Ferguson.'

'What do you want, McKenzie?'

'Mr Curran's doing well.'

'He'll do better tomorrow with Taylor in the box.'

'That's my problem. Can you not slow him down a bit?'

'Why?'

'I'm having trouble talking the rest of the jury round to my point of view.'

'They think Taylor did it?'

'Of course he done it. But there's a squad of holy joes in the jury room. Eye-for-an-eye bunch and they're mad to hang somebody.'

'I told you. I want a not guilty verdict.'

'All it takes is for one juror to hold out. There's no majority verdict. It's unanimous or nothing. You'll get a retrial. Different jury.'

'Yes, but you won't be on that jury, McKenzie, will you? I put you on this one to get a not guilty verdict.'

'You put me on the jury? You never told me that before.'

'You think I can't put my hand on a jury list? And I tell you what else I can put my hand on. The licence for that pub of yours. Or the cargo manifest for the bootleg gin you bring in from Liverpool. You think you'll stay in business long if I decide that another man could make a better job of your public house and that bonehouse you have out the back?'

'I get the point, Mr Ferguson.'

'Then go back to your hotel and get that jury out of bed and explain to them how the world works. Tell them to leave justice to God. He's got plenty to go around. It's in short supply in this town.'

McKenzie threw his cigarette into the gutter where it quenched in the incessant rain. He walked off into the light cast by a streetlight and into the darkness beyond. Water drummed on the stretched canvas above Ferguson's head. The headlights of a police tender swept the end of the street, then moved on, but he felt himself shrink back into the doorway behind him.

Ferguson had known the dead pimp, Harry Coogan. He had defended him in the crown court against charges of procurement in the year before he was murdered. Coogan a black marketeer, sharp-dressed, good-looking, leering from the back seat of a taxi after the charges had been dropped. *Anything you want, Mr Ferguson. Just give me a bell. Anything.* Ferguson felt once again the presence of Coogan and his female charges gathered on the pavement opposite, their whispering and beckoning, his fellows in that shadowed mews.

The rain had cleared the following morning. The basalt mountains were fogged and the air was warm and still. Ferguson walked to the court buildings through the Botanic Gardens, past the giant leaf ferns and trees of the palm house, still and primal in the moist glasshouse air. Patricia waited for him at the northern entrance to the gardens.

'Does your father know that you're not going to school?'

'Do you think he misses anything that happens in that courtroom? I think he regards this as part of my education.'

'He wants you to understand something of the law.'

'Is that what it is?'

Ferguson didn't answer. He didn't know why Curran wanted his daughter in the public gallery. He didn't know why Patricia felt it necessary to be there. He saw her looking out over the crowd gathering in the court precinct and he studied her face. The deep-set eyes, her father's mouth, downturned at the corners. There's not much of the mother's blood in her, he thought. She is her father's child.

It would be a long day. Taylor was to be in the witness box. They would see him cornered. They were down to the bare bones of the case. A man was to stand in front of others and attest to the truth or otherwise of his doings in the world. Ferguson wondered if this was the reason that Curran wanted his daughter in the courtroom. To see her father's work among the fallen. Esther had spoken to him about it as he left that morning, calling to him from a darkened bedroom. He stood in the door and heard her stir.

'Will Patricia be there?' she asked.

'I think so,' he said.

'It's not something I would wish a child of mine to see,' she said.

'What part of it?' Ferguson asked.

'Any of it,' she said, 'any of it.'

The three final prosecution witnesses preceded Taylor into the box. Dr J. B. Firth told the court that the bloodstains on Taylor's clothing belonged to blood group O. The victim was blood group O, as was Taylor. Curran asked him about the human hairs which were found on the shoulders of Taylor's overcoat. Firth said that fifteen hairs had been found, all belonging to Mary McGowan. The hairs were bloodstained. Curran raised the matter of wax polish found on the soles of the victim's shoes, Lyon's wax polish, which was used by the Taylors but not by the McGowans.

Newsagent George Clarke was called to say that Taylor had not collected his newspaper on the morning of the murder, despite Taylor's assertion that he had, providing himself with an alibi. The next witness was a friend of Taylor's, Billie Booth. Taylor had told the police interrogators that he had borrowed money from Booth and so had no need of money on the day of the murder. Booth denied that he had ever lent money to Taylor. The final witness was the owner of Morrison's pub, where Taylor drank. Alexander Morrison stated that Taylor had asked him for a loan, although he omitted to say that the request had come on the morning of the murder. Ferguson thought that Curran did not look pleased.

Hanna and his junior, Fox, did not prolong their cross-examination. They pressed Clarke, but he was adamant that Taylor had not picked up his newspaper. Ferguson nudged Patricia when the prison doctor, Girvan, came into the box. Curran had him describe the deep scratches on Taylor's face when he examined him, but Fox ignored the scratches. He asked a single question.

'Is Taylor a perfectly normal man?'

'He appeared perfectly normal.'

Patricia starting to understand. Hanna trying to set up Taylor as a normal man. The act of murdering Mary McGowan was not normal, therefore Taylor could not have carried it out.

The court clerk called Taylor's name. He stood up. Lily made a gesture towards him, her veil stirring. Taylor turned to her. His smile warm. He looked as if he might lay a hand on her arm. *Be strong.* But the usher guided him towards the box. Looking confident as he took the Bible in his hand. *Babyface killer.* The newspapers afterwards describing him as 'confident', 'assured'.

Patricia later told Hilary Douglas that Taylor was like an actor in the box. He was playing a role and that role was innocence.

'Did he play it well?' Hilary asked.

'He did. He played it very well,' Patricia said. 'Mr Hanna gave him his lines.'

Hilary was to remember the conversation three years later when Iain Hay Gordon was put in the witness box during his trial for the murder of Patricia. Hilary wondering what Patricia would have said about Gordon repudiating the confession he had given to Chief Inspector Capstick. Gordon nervy, hard to read. Hilary imagined dropping her voice to tell Patricia that he was a homo, laughing at the expression on Patricia's face when she heard the word.

'What is your name?'

'Robert Taylor.'

'Age?'

'Twenty-one.'

'And your employer until recently?'

'Mr Barrett of Sunnyside Street.'

'You have recently become engaged to a young lady named Elizabeth Jones.'

'Yes.' Taylor's eyes going to Lily in the front of the public gallery. Lily lifting a tremulous hand.

'Pure bloody ham,' Patricia whispered.

Hanna set about constructing the case for Taylor. Taylor leaving home at 9.45 a.m. Buying his newspaper. Going to see Billie Booth about money. This account placing him elsewhere when Mary McGowan was murdered.

'He's getting to the blood now,' Ferguson said. Hanna rearranging his papers on the bench in front of him, looking absent-minded, avuncular. He looked at Taylor over the top of his glasses.

'On your coat and other garments traces of blood were found. Would you tell the judge and the jury how that blood got on them?'

'It got on them through my nose bleeding on Good Friday and the Monday before.'

'Where were you when your nose began to bleed?'

Patricia felt a kind of wonderment. That they should construct such a dance around the dead woman's blood. She had entered her father's study the previous evening. He had been studying texts and papers on blood. The groups and platelets. There were monochrome photographs of blood-spatter at crime scenes, patterned across ceilings and household furnishings. There were dark poolings under dead bodies. She read the papers until night fell around her. Lost in the dread science, her father's daughter. Passive and transfer stains. Arterial spurting. Cast-off stains. Impact spatter. Unaware that in time her own blood would be the subject of similar attention.

Taylor at Hanna's prompting went on to describe the angle of blood drips from his nose, the downward trajectory that might explain the stains to various parts of his clothing. Taylor breezy and articulate. How the blood got on his overcoat. How the blood got on his socks. The nature and frequency of his nosebleeds. Ferguson could see McKenzie nudging the other jurors, urging them towards Hanna's arguments. Ferguson thinking *Don't bloody overdo it, McKenzie.* He could see Hanna working the rhythms into his speech, the street preacher's flourishes. Question and answer. Statement and retort.

'Did you know Mrs McGowan?'

'Yes.'

'Had you worked for her?'

'Yes.'

'Did you see her on the sixteenth of April?'

'No.'

'Did you make any attack on her?'

'No.'

'That day or any other day?'

'No.'

'Did you attempt to throttle her?'

'No.'

'Did you kick her?'

'No.'

'Did you go into her house on that day?'

'No.'

Watching the prisoner in the dock, Patricia was reminded of Sunday school and the scuffed and foxed texts that were passed around. Tales of children who misbehaved and accepted their chastisement and were returned to God. There were stories of children that told the truth against overwhelming odds, their voices ringing out in the presence of soldiers and tyrants, and Taylor reminded her of such a child. She thought of him illustrated in pastel colours, his voice clear and piping. Undaunted. Hanna returned to his bench and she saw her father stand up, black-suited and wigged, proxy to some old malice, his mouth downturned, waiting until the court fell silent before he spoke, his voice dry and uninflected, looking down at his notes as though a tally and account of Taylor's wrongdoing was written there and had fallen due to be paid.

'Mr Taylor, you were to be married.'

'I was.'

'And you required twelve pounds and nine shillings to pay

for the wedding cars, and you required three or four pounds for the ring.'

'Yes.'

'And in your possession you had not more than five pounds?'

'Yes.'

'You lied to the police when you said that your friend Booth owed you money. You lied, did you not, Mr Taylor?'

'Yes.'

'Why did you lie?'

'I didn't want the police to know I was borrowing money when they were seeing me.'

'Why?'

'Well they were around seeing me about an assault that had been committed.'

Ferguson could hear signs of the coaching that Taylor had been given, the lawyer's cadences of the sentences, *an assault that had been committed.* Curran breaking down his story by breaking down his language.

'I say again. Why?'

'Well, it would look bad for me at the time.'

'Is it because it would give you reason for assaulting Mrs McGowan?'

'Yes.'

'So when the police came to you it occurred to you that the fact that you had tried to borrow money that morning would be against you.'

'Yes.'

'It might lead the police to believe that you had assaulted Mrs McGowan?'

'Yes.'

Taylor looked over at Hanna. Three uses of the word yes in a row. He seemed uncertain of what he had given his assent to. Hanna's eyes were on Curran. All eyes in the courtroom were on Curran. He placed his notes on the dais to his left and moved to the front of his bench. Taylor turned his head away from Hanna, his attention drawn to Curran against his will it seemed. Curran waited until the whole courtroom was stilled. He stood in front of them, his black robes gathered about him like an orator in some cold senate.

'We will now come to the matter of blood,' he said.

Patricia leaned over to Ferguson. He could feel her breath on his cheek.

'It's a sin to tell a lie.'

'What?'

'The Bobby Breen song.' Ferguson remembering Esther at Glenravel Street barracks naming the song.

Curran's cross-examination was harsh and lyric. It was a song of blood, a blaming canticle sung out in the courtroom.

'Why did you tell the police that the stains on your coat were caused by paint?'

'Well it could have been paint . . . I thought it was paint.'

'Why?'

'Because I work with paint.'

'Did it occur to you that having bloodstains on your coat would be against you in connection with the assault on Mrs McGowan?'

'I didn't think about it. The police said they were bloodstains. I didn't know it was blood.'

Taylor's syntax falling apart.

'Did you remember at the time that your nose had been

bleeding the day before?'

'I never thought about it.'

'Has your nose bled since?'

'No. It's only when I'm painting that it bleeds.'

'Have you had medical attention at any time for your nose?'

'No.'

'Can you explain how the blood got on the shoulder of your overcoat?'

'No.'

'All this nose-bleeding happened the day before?'

'Yes.'

'And did it not occur to you to tell the truth about it?'

'No.'

'Did you know the blood on your coat and trousers was blood?'

'I suppose I did.'

Taylor turning sullen now. Something of the cur about him. Lily glad that he wouldn't be coming home to her. She knew what happened when Taylor felt that people were against him.

'Just explain how that splash of blood could have got down to your foot from your nose bleeding.'

'It could have dropped down when I was in the lavatory.'

'Did you notice any splash on your right leg?'

'I knew it was dropping down.'

'If you knew that then why did you not tell the police that the stain on your sock and foot was caused by your nose bleeding?'

'I didn't think of that.'

'I see. Now how do you account for the fact that the blood-stained hairs on your coat match those on Mrs McGowan's head?'

Taylor couldn't account for it. A silence fell on the courtroom. He looked to his father, then he looked to Lily. He couldn't see her face through the black veil but her hands were clasped in her lap and he looked at them as though she held some pale, cold truth there.

'I don't know,' he said.

'The hairs, Mr Taylor,' the judge said. 'Can you tell the court how Mrs McGowan's bloodstained hairs were found on your person?'

'I don't know.' Taylor hadn't expected the judge to repeat Curran's question. He didn't think it was fair for Curran and the judge to gang up on him like this. He had already told Curran he didn't know how the hairs on his coat matched the victim's hair. If you didn't know something nobody could make you know it.

Curran waited until the jury had absorbed the judge's intervention, then asked his final question.

'How do you account for the fact that one of the bloodstains on your coat was still wet?'

'I don't know how it was wet.' Taylor looking sulky now. A blamed-in-the-wrong, childish air to him. Curran said nothing more. He turned away from the accused man and stood facing the rear wall of the courtroom. Patricia wanted to tell him not to do it. That he didn't need to use this kind of shabby theatrics.

'He's gone a bit too far,' Ferguson said in a whisper, 'just a bit. It hardly matters.'

'You may step down, Mr Taylor,' the judge said. Taylor walked back to the dock. He looked like an old man now, a pavement shuffler in an oversized suit. As the court rose McKenzie looked in Ferguson's direction.

'Why is that man looking at you?' Patricia said.

'Which one?'

'The man in the jury.'

'He's the foreman of the jury. His name's McKenzie. From the Shankill Road.'

'Oh my God, Harry.'

'What?'

'You haven't nobbled the jury, have you?'

'Why would I do that?'

'To make sure that Father wins.'

'It would be nice if I could. But I don't think he needs me, do you? Besides, the jury all look like holy joes. Hard to corrupt that sort.'

Outside the courthouse Patricia nudged Ferguson. 'The jury's not the only holy joes around here. Look.'

Desmond Curran was standing at the front gate of the courthouse. He was handing out leaflets to the departing crowd. Some of them laughed but many took leaflets. It was a city of pamphleteers and zealots, and people liked to feel that they were attending to the undercurrents.

'Does Father ever say anything to you about Desmond?' Patricia said.

'No,' Ferguson said.

'That's a lie, Harry. I can tell when you're lying, you know. I'm probably one of the few that can. Father isn't happy about all of the religious stuff. But I think it bothers Mother more. Deep down. Desmond thinks that we should pursue each other with loving relentlessness.'

'I think you'll find the the pamphlet tells you to pursue another's salvation with loving relentlessness.'

'Really? I like the idea of being pursued with loving relentlessness.'

'I'm sure it will happen, Patricia.'

'You think so, Harry? Honestly, I thought nunhood awaited me. Looks like Desmond's got rid of all his handouts. Here he comes.'

Desmond shook Ferguson's hand.

'Good afternoon, Mr Ferguson.'

'Desmond.'

'Are you going to say hello to me, Desmond?'

'I was going to ask you why you aren't at school.'

'The trial of the century, Desmond. It's instructive. I'm getting a rounded education.' Desmond leaning forward, a sandy-haired, earnest figure, his hands clasped behind his back, striking a donnish pose. Esther had commented on his good looks. When Ferguson saw him he thought of the SS prisoners he had seen at Nuremberg. The fine-boned Aryan faces, death's-head on the tunic collar. Walking alone among the captured, holding themselves apart, loyal still to some profane corps.

'You'd better get home. You know what happens with Mother when you're not on the bus.'

'I didn't ask,' Ferguson said, 'forgive me, Desmond. How is your mother?'

'Mad as a bloody hatter,' Patricia said. Desmond turned on her. For a moment Ferguson thought that he was going to strike her. Patricia lowered her eyes.

'I'm sorry, Desmond,' she said, 'my big mouth. That wasn't fair.'

Ten

FEBRUARY 1961

'Do you remember the Taylor trial, Mrs Curran?'

'That would be Lady Curran to you, you whelp.'

Ferguson waited in silence. Doris walked in the storied dark. The nurses said that characters came and went. They stepped into the circle of light, they spoke their piece and then were gone back into the shadow. They were travellers and did not stay long in one place. Madness was a story, a ghast yarn spun in the firelight. They swarmed over her mind for days on end. You had to ignore them, Ferguson thought. If you ignored them long enough they would go away and allow Doris to emerge, kindly, nodding, an elderly woman in a flannelette dressing gown.

'Taylor was the chap that murdered poor Mrs McGowan,' Doris said.

'Yes.'

'A bad lot.'

'He was. He did a lot of harm.'

'I went down to the trial,' Doris said. 'I never did go to the courthouse but that day I thought to myself, why not? But when I got there they were queued all the way to the City Hall. I couldn't get in.'

'You should have asked someone. You were the Attorney General's wife.'

'I didn't think of it then, Mr Ferguson. There were such a lot of people. What the hell do you want to know about that for?'

Normally there was time to take on the change in her voice, Doris slipping away, stepping back into the shadows. This time the change was instant. The voice was rich, mannish, sardonic. When Ferguson turned to Doris, her eyes met his and he took a step backwards. *Dark blue, very sharp.* Doris sat forward, her legs apart, her elbows resting on her thighs.

'Judge Curran said he didn't trust you on the Taylor case. He said he didn't know what you were up to. Too slippery for your own good. Harry is a means to an end, the Judge said, and I'll be done with him in the heel of the hunt.'

'Who did he say this to?'

'To Doris, man, who else would he say it to? He scared Doris. Don't be scared of him, I says to Doris. She was easy feared, Doris, in them days, and Patricia had her tortured. Never mind, Patricia, I says, me and you'll have some sport with her, by and by. Did you ever go sporting with the lasses, Harry?'

'What do you mean?'

'Sporting with the lasses under the arches in Whitechapel. And after I was took to the asylum at Broadmoor.'

'Same as Doris.'

'Same as Doris. Dr Meyer spoke to me there. He says the causes of madness are as follows. Intemperance. Vice. Poverty. Fright. Religious Excitement. Exposure to Hot Climates. Which of them answers befits me? If indeed you think me mad at all.'

'I don't know.'

'Do you think me in my right mind?'

'I can't answer that.'

'Your own married wife could answer for thee, I think she's

a lass has given many's a man a run for his money.' There was a half-smile on her face. The voice delinquent, mocking.

'Did you?' Ferguson said.

'Did I what?'

'Did you and Doris have sport with Patricia? Did you sport with her in her bedroom where the bloodstain was found on the floor? Did you carry her body outside into the trees?'

'Out in the trees?'

'That's where the Judge found her.'

'The Judge always finds you, no matter where you hide.' Doris passed her hand over her face. When she took it away she was an old woman again. The hand she had passed over her face, now weak and palsied, fell to her side.

'I'm very tired,' she said.

'I'll call a nurse.'

'Thank you. That would be kind.'

Ferguson walked over to the door and rang the bell. He lifted a rug and put it over Doris's knees. She did not respond. When the nurse came she looked at Ferguson.

'The poor thing's done out. You should have let her be, mister.'

The nurse helped Doris to her feet and linked her to the door, Doris dragging her feet. As she reached the door she lifted her head and glanced at Ferguson.

A woman standing in the exercise yard. She is nude. There are scapulars about her neck.

Eleven

JULY 1949

Hilary would wait for Patricia at Oxford Street bus station to hear what had happened at the trial that day. They would go out the back of the station. Hilary always had cigarettes, Dunhills or Black Cats. They'd sit in among the maintenance vehicles and tow trucks, sharing a cigarette. Hilary had a way of finding the hidden places of the city, the derelict canal banks and building sites. She knew the rusted-through locks and bent railings, squirming into old factory spaces and waterworks. She took Patricia to a Quaker graveyard in Stranmillis, ivy and nettles growing through the vaults and tilted headstones. Hilary and other fifth years would meet Wesley boys there after evening service in the wintertime. Hilary sometimes let them 'go too far', telling Patricia about it afterwards, her talk smutty and detailed.

Patricia had waited for her just inside the gates. She didn't want to go in with the boys, anonymous figures passing her in the dark, the girls waiting for them among the bent stones and scrub growth. Sometimes there'd be sounds from the graveyard interior, small cries and moans that made her start. Waiting until Hilary came out, straightening her blazer, her stockings laddered.

One night Hilary made Patricia wait longer than usual, Patricia shivering, pulling her coat around her. She was about to call out when Hilary came out with a tall boy that Patricia recognised as one of the Wesley rugby team. As he ducked past Patricia she saw Hilary watch after him, drawing the back of her hand across her mouth, something feral in the look, a base appetite sated.

Hilary couldn't get enough of the trial. She made Patricia describe the demeanour of the witnesses, what they were wearing, the procedures and the ritual, the wigs and gowns and processional entrances. She would buy the early edition of the Telegraph and read passages of evidence aloud, getting Patricia to add details – whether the witness was sweating or fearful, if the judge looked sternly over his glasses at the defendant, did the public gallery gasp and turn to each other for comfort at some shocking passage of evidence, Hilary caught up in the sweep of the trial, the whole strange and graphic tumult of it. She wanted dramatics, the accused collapsing in the box sobbing, judges thundering from the bench.

'The noonday sun blazed down on Newington as the killer known as Babyface Taylor swaggered towards the quiet house. Sweet little old lady Mary McGowan went about her day's business, unaware that fate had singled her out for murder most foul. Taylor had one thing on his mind.'

'Put a sock in it, Hilary,' Patricia said, 'you've watched too many cowboy films. It's not like that.'

But Hilary's fictions had an authority of their own and they stayed with Patricia. In this version Taylor a drifter in some western dreamtime. Pacing the dusty street, the sun beating down, the hallucinatory noontime glare. Other times she made him a Chicago gangster, John Dillinger, gunned down outside the Biograph, giving him an allure he didn't have. Patricia wanted to tell Hilary that Taylor wasn't like that, given to a killer's terse monosyllables, the long-distance stare, seeing beyond the moment. There were no flat existential perspectives, the camera panning across deserted landscapes on the edge of town. The two girls smoking in the bus yard, tar-smelling, sticky with spilled oil. Finding their way into the back of a broken-down bus, the smell of warm leatherette, cigarette smoke hanging in the air, late-afternoon languor in the summer, Hilary's stories taking on an air of foretelling, of a future rife with sudden death.

'Your father's the lawman. He rides into town, makes things safe for the townsfolk.'

'He's not really like that.'

'Of course he is. The strong silent type.'

'He gambles, Hilary.'

'Does he? That's fantastic. Makes him even more interesting. Sitting at the card table with the gunslinger, his face betrayed no emotion. He knew what he was dealing with. They all did.'

'Don't be ridiculous.'

'Bet he carries a silver derringer.'

'Hardly. There's not much need of silver derringers at the Reform Club.'

'I suppose so. What sort of gambling does he do?'

'Cards mostly, I think. Though he might do horses as well. I've heard him on the telephone with this man Hughes who is a bookmaker.'

'Do tell all.' Hilary leaning forward confidentially. It was what she liked, the adolescent sphere of sharing, confidential asides. Girls telling each other everything. Patricia saw it all the time, girls walking home from school, their heads together, the telling of secrets, the sweet lore of adolescence. All the girls in school feeling the confidential undercurrent, the deep tug of it, the whispered conversation in corridors, the late-evening telephone calls. Hilary liked to use made-up words, a coded and allusive vocabulary of the heart. It was important that everything to do with feelings was kept secret, that an aura was created. A boy she liked was svelte. Girl rivals were hussies.

'Mother and Father don't talk very much. Mother's a bit highly strung. Sometimes she locks herself in the bedroom and won't come out. Father hides the key.'

'Poor Patricia. What does Desmond do?'

'Desmond ignores it all.'

'He's quite handsome, your Desmond.'

'Hilary, don't tell me you're sweet on Desmond as well?'

'What do you mean by as well?'

'As well as the entire Wesley rugby team. As well as the hockey team and the men's gymnastic association. Do you want me to go on?'

'I see what you mean. I am a bit loose with my affections, aren't I? A girl of easy virtue.'

'A girl of not much virtue at all.'

Hilary told Patricia things that she did with boys. How she dealt with the hussies, turning one against the other, leaving a trail of hints and half-truths for them. She lay down on the back seat of the bus and put her head in Patricia's lap.

'We have to pick some svelte thing out for you. You're going positively nunnish.'

'I'm saving my womanhood, Hilary. I'm being picky.'

'Meaning I'm not? You have an old heart, my dear. I think

we're going to have to find you a mature man.'

Patricia had gone with some of the Wesley boys but she found herself thinking beyond the moment, seeing herself walking home, submitting to their callow fumblings.

'I want someone to make love to me. I don't want to be groped in the shrubbery.'

'Where do you want to be groped?' Hilary lifted her head from Patricia's lap. She knew that Patricia was holding back. It was all right to have deep dark secrets as long as they were brought out into the light eventually. Those were the rules of the game.

Patricia said that her mother liked to have her hair brushed. Only Patricia was allowed into her room. She would lie on the bed beside her mother to comb her hair, still long and worn in a bun. Patricia knew how to undo the pins, lay out the hanks, working her way into the lustres, listening to her mother's talk of herself and the hair, the teaspoon of vinegar in the rinse water, knew the hair as a swirling, nuanced thing. She had a dressing table with a mirror on either side and she watched herself while Patricia brushed. She had a brush set with silver backs and tortoiseshell.

'Patricia, you're getting a décolletage, you really are,' Hilary said.

'Father always calls me Patricia in a way that makes me feel like the accused standing in the dock, ready to be transported off to some dread shore.'

Patricia told Hilary that when she was ten her father had taken her to Whiteabbey police station. While her father was talking to the sergeant a constable asked her if she would like to see the cells. He told her to go into one, which she did. The cell was whitewashed with a plain bed and the policeman closed the door and said for her to sit on the bed.

'What did you do?'

'Screamed. He opened the door double quick.'

Hilary's father had men he went golfing with. The chaps, Hilary called them. They made Hilary laugh, until one of the chaps gave her a lift home from school one evening.

'He put his rotten hand on my knee,' Hilary said. 'He is a perv and a creep. I couldn't imagine Harry Ferguson doing anything like that. I saw him in his uniform when he came home from the war. He looked a whizz in it.'

Patricia had come across her father's uniform in a closet in the spare bedroom. The tunic. The belt. The smells of starch, of oil worked into the leather. Brasso used on the buttons. She remembered finding her father's wig in the hallway, the wig in its dented tin hatbox. Patricia danced into the dining room with the wig askew on her head, then turned to each of them in turn and said, *I judge you, I judge you, I judge you.*

Hilary knew that Patricia was holding back but she did not know that she was thinking about Harry Ferguson. Ferguson was Father's friend but he had something brutal about him. You could see it in his eyes. People were afraid of Ferguson although she had never heard him raise his voice. She could smell his cologne from the sleeve of her cardigan where she had pressed against him in the courtroom. He wore a wrist watch with a gold metal strap and a signet ring on his right hand. There was fine, reddish hair on the back of his hands. Patricia thought they would be strong and agile. There was something knowing about Ferguson's hands. She found herself thinking about them independent of him. What a hand does. Weighing and grasping. She imagined grips and holds, deft touches.

Hilary sat up. She lit another cigarette and handed it to Patricia. Patricia remembered the night she had stood outside the house with Ferguson, taking a pull on his cigarette. Looking back there seemed to be ritual to the encounter, gestures that seemed deliberated over, as though coming to them out of some deep faith, the sensual rites, a man and a woman standing together in the night.

'Don't tell me who it is now,' Hilary said, 'but tell me some time, agreed?'

'Scouts' honour,' Patricia said.

'Is it someone svelte?' Hilary said.

'Very svelte,' Patricia said.

Hilary put her head back in Patricia's lap. The sun was at its zenith, the girls feeling languid, unpicking their blouses where the heat made the fabric stick to their skin, passing the cigarette to and fro, the scene fading out as the sun moved behind the vaulted bus station roof, taking with it the day's heat, the lost girlhoods.

*

'I'm going to be convicted,' Taylor said, 'they're going to put a rope around my neck and string me up like a rat and then they're going to put me in a grave and pour quicklime over me. How long does quicklime take to dissolve a body, Mr Lunn? Not long. A week maybe.'

'Steady yourself, Robert,' Lunn said. But he was worried. Curran's cross-examination of Taylor had been devastating.

'We erected a good defence insofar as you can make a silk purse out of a sow's ear, but we didn't plan on Curran tearing it to shreds.'

'Curran knew his duty in the matter,' Hanna said. 'There is considerable disquiet regarding his behaviour.'

'We opened the bloody door for him,' Lunn said, 'all he had to do was walk through.'

'People are starting to wonder if Curran is the man they thought he was.'

'Two weeks tops,' Taylor said. 'The bone would take longer.' Absorbed in the mechanics of the burial, the chemical fire, what it was like to be consumed.

'There is no question of your being hanged,' Lunn said.

'There was no question of Curran eating me alive until he done it,' Taylor said. 'That's what you told me.'

'I thought Ferguson would knock some sense into him.'

'I'd wait and see. Harry usually has something up his sleeve.'

'For Curran's sake he'd better have.'

'Never mind Curran's sake,' Taylor said. 'What about my sake?'

Lunn had arranged to meet Hanna in the Reform Club later that night, following a visit to his client in prison. He met Curran in the lobby and Curran inclined his head. Lunn found Hanna in the smoking room with Ellis Harvey.

'I met Curran on the way in. He threw me the nod. He's a cool customer, I'll give him that,' Lunn said.

'I think we had better prepare for a guilty verdict tomorrow,' Hanna said. 'A guilty verdict and an appeal.'

'Police reserves have been called up,' Harvey said, 'but they won't be able to contain it if it spills over. We'll have to let the mob have its head for the night, I'm afraid.'

'It's this heat,' Lunn said. 'The place is primed and ready to blow.'

Lunn had walked across the city by the Crumlin Road, coming past Cambrai Street, Crimea Street, the Oldpark Road, turning down Agnes Street on to the Shankill. The streetlights had been extinguished.

'You're ready to sum up tomorrow?' Harvey said.

'I'll do what I can,' Hanna said, 'if you can keep a lid on the town and Ferguson can put a curb on Curran.'

'He hasn't much hope of putting a curb on Curran if he can't keep a curb on that.'

They followed Lunn's eyes. Esther Ferguson was crossing the bar. She was wearing a blue blouse in slub silk and a black pencil skirt. Her eyes were fixed on the bar, her lips moving as though she was uttering a prayer, an incantation of warding and protecting, the words that would carry her across the floor, other eyes watching her.

'She's no asset to Ferguson, that's for sure,' Lunn said. 'I hear tell she's there for the asking.'

'We all have our weaknesses,' Harvey said. 'There's many a man in this town would have to pack his bags if a light was shone into dark corners.'

'Here comes another one that's for the fairies,' Lunn said. Doris Curran crossed the room and took Esther by the arm.

'I think I see Harry coming, Mrs Ferguson,' she said. 'Perhaps we ought to freshen up before he comes in.' She put her arm through Esther's and led her towards the ladies.

'The blind leading the blind,' Lunn said.

'How's that?' Hanna said.

'I hear tell she's high-strung. Surprised to see her out at all.'

'Heads down. Here comes Harry.' Ferguson crossed the room without looking at their table.

'Off for a game of snooker with Curran,' Lunn said. 'I hope he's going to have a word in his ear.'

'If it wasn't for Ferguson and his kind, this place would have collapsed long ago,' Harvey said.

'He's only useful as long as he does his job,' Hanna said.

Ferguson saw Hanna and Lunn in conversation with Ellis Harvey. He walked on through the bar and dining room, taking stock of the gathered groups and cliques, powerful men and their supplicants. There were bridge and canasta games being played in adjunct rooms. He climbed the stairs to the billiard room but Curran wasn't there. He went into the long room where a band was playing muted songs of the pre-war era, couples dancing, lost in complex nostalgias for a time that never was. Ferguson listened to the music, leaning against the wall. He thought that Esther might have been on the dancefloor, held in a man's arms, and knew that he shouldn't be there. There was a codex of the unsaid. Heartbreak came with its own rules. She was not to be shamed. She had kissed his cheek when he left the house that morning and she had not been there when he returned. The fledgling intimacies of courtship were all that were left to them. He raised his hand to his face where her lips had brushed his skin.

He left the ballroom and went down the stairs, people starting to drift home early as though a curfew had been set. He asked the porter if he had seen Esther. The porter told him that his wife had left.

As he went down the front steps Ferguson saw Harvey in front of him, walking slowly on a cane. Harvey had contracted polio in the Middle East and had been left with a deformed leg. Ferguson caught up with him.

'It's not a night for walking home.'

'There aren't any taxis. I'll manage.'

'I don't have the car with me.'

'I'm fine, Ferguson.'

'No you're not. Not on a night like this. I'll walk with you.' Harvey shrugged. Ferguson took off his jacket and loosened his tie. Feeling the heat from the pavements and the walls, his shirt sticking to his back. He thought of Esther's kiss that morning, the light sour touch of a wife's kiss like sweat drying between the shoulderblades. Down a side street he saw the remnants of a bonfire, men standing in the darkness behind it.

'It doesn't feel like the town I grew up in,' Ferguson said, the heat of the night changing the fabric of the place, something foetid hanging in the air.

'I was in Egypt during the war,' Harvey said. 'Cairo. Sometimes the place would go quiet like this. You never knew why.' The seething city hushed at nightfall, eyes watching from the alleyways, the narrow passages, the faithful called to prayer. Harvey seeing his city like some eastern metropolis, assassins at large in the souk, robed figures.

'Curran has placed himself in some jeopardy,' Harvey said.

'And me along with him.'

'I didn't say that.'

'You didn't have to.'

'What is your thinking on the verdict tomorrow?'

'I don't know.' Ferguson could see McKenzie's face. Jowled, corruptible. He tried to picture a jury room with McKenzie as advocate, directing the others towards a not guilty verdict. Reminding them of their responsibilities, urging them towards the bigger picture.

'It's tough when the defendant is guilty as sin,' he said.

'And his prosecutor is determined to see him with a rope around his neck.'

'I am Mr Curran's adviser, not his master.'

At the museum building Harvey asked Ferguson to come in.

'We're in the process of installing a new exhibit. A mummy. You might be intrigued.'

'I've never seen one.'

'It's a female. Somewhere between twenty and thirty years of age.'

Harvey unlocked the museum side door and they went in. He led Ferguson through dimlit passages with the sense that they were working their way inwards, towards some sanctum, a chambered grave with pottery shards, traces of sacrifice. The mummy was in a side room strewn with wood shavings and they had to walk between packing cases to reach it. She was enclosed in a casket of wood painted with the likeness of an upper-caste Egyptian woman with a straight fringe and eyes highlighted in kohl. Harvey took one end of the wooden lid, Ferguson took the other and they lifted it off.

The mummy's name was Takabuti and she had been disinterred in Egypt and brought by ship to the city and they had unwrapped her and now she was in a white linen shroud. Her skin was black with age and leathern. Her nose had drawn inwards and her lips were shrunken to a tight ragged line stretched over her teeth. Her tow-coloured hair clung to her skull.

Ferguson had expected a royal figure, an arch Nile princess, not this tiny crouched form under a linen wrap. He imagined her in her tomb. Stored about her would have been jars containing her preserved viscera. Wrapped foodstuffs and unguents prepared for a journey.

Her eyes were in shadow until Harvey moved the lamp. The eyelid skin had shrunk and discoloured to give the impression that her eyes were open and staring and Ferguson moved out of the sightless glare.

'It gave me a shock when I saw her first,' Harvey said. 'You think about all the old superstitions.'

Ferguson did not want to look the mummy in the face again. The head lay to one side, the two men fixed in its unholy glare. He had seen dead bodies before, the roads and ditches of northern France littered with them. But this was a different kind of death, the eyes that of some unholy coquette.

'You'd have been better off leaving that thing in the ground where it belongs,' he said.

'It's only an artefact,' Harvey said.

'It's a bit more than that,' Ferguson said. One blackened hand lay outside the linen covering, crooked as though it beckoned, and as he moved away Ferguson brushed it with his own hand and swore. There was sweat on his forehead and his shirt stuck to his body.

'You look like you need a drink,' Harvey said.

*

Ferguson sat down on a leather chair in Harvey's office. Harvey went to the window and opened it but the air that came in was still and warm. They listened for the sounds of riot from the north and west of the city but nothing stirred. The city waiting. Harvey poured gin.

'Curran is a gambler,' he said.

'So you tell me.'

'And I'm telling you again. A man can gamble when what he puts on the table belongs to him. Not otherwise.'

'So what is Curran gambling with?'

'This.' Harvey was looking out over the city. 'The place is smouldering, Ferguson, and it will burn some day. But not on my watch. I want to make that clear. It will not happen on my watch.'

'Nobody wants to see the city burn.'

'Then get Curran to ease back on his summing up tomorrow. Give the jury something to hang an innocent verdict on.'

'It's too late for that. Besides, Curran doesn't do what I tell him to do. You've got that one the wrong way round, Mr Harvey. I've done what I can.'

Harvey remained standing, looking out over the city, his face pinched and vehement, his knuckles white around the glass, as though he expected cohorts of the dead to rise out of the darksome streets and ride down innocent and guilty alike.

Twelve

MARCH 1961

Ferguson flew into Heathrow ahead of a storm blown down from the North Channel, the last plane out before the first snow, the plane's landing lights flashing off the underside of the laden clouds, snowfall in the distance, fathom-deep sheets of white swept overland from the sea. The aircraft bucked in the turbulence, the airframe flexed and groaned. Ferguson looking out the window without seeing.

At Heathrow the gritters were out on the runways. Ice particles from the aircraft wings swirled in the apron lights. By the time Ferguson left the airport in a taxi there was sleet blowing under the motorway lights, few cars, traffic coming out of the south looking migrant, gone north into a long wintering.

Ferguson hadn't seen Chief Inspector John Capstick since Iain Hay Gordon had been convicted for the murder of Patricia Curran, but he had followed his high-profile cases in the newspapers. The murders of John and Phoebe Harries, the murder of Edwina Taylor. Capstick's autobiography, Given in Evidence, had been published in 1960, giving accounts of his famous cases. The tone of the book is folksy and upbeat, the hard-pressed copper hampered by red tape in his pursuit of 'chummy', nevertheless managing to catch the miscreant. Ferguson picking up the undertones of planted evidence, false confessions, suspects beaten in cold station cell blocks, blood on the floor. He remembered Gordon's supposed confession to the murder of Patricia, the coached feel to it, the use of copper's argot.

Each chapter of Given in Evidence introduces a new case and the chapter headings are stylised and lurid. 'Blood on the Moon'. 'Little Girl Lost'. Tales of provincial child abductors, cheating wives and jilted lovers, the faithless and the renegade. Ferguson knew that Capstick had a reputation for bringing a suspect into an interrogation room alone and emerging with a guilty plea. He had forced the confession from Gordon for Patricia's murder by threatening to reveal to Gordon's mother that he was a homosexual.

Capstick had retired but he arranged to meet Ferguson at Scotland Yard. Ferguson was brought to an upstairs office with carpet on the floor and panelled walls. Capstick stood up from a leather-bound armchair when Ferguson came in. He was a big man, dressed in a worsted suit and floral tie. A black homburg sat on the desk. Ferguson could smell hair lotion, a strong scent with a rank undertone. Capstick was sixty-five but looked vigorous and cunning. He told Ferguson to sit.

'You don't mind if I smoke?'

'Fire ahead, Chief Inspector.' Ferguson waited while Capstick filled his pipe and lit it, drawing out each movement, deliberating over it.

'You use that in interrogations, Chief Inspector?'

'It was always said you had a quick mind, Mr Ferguson. Yes, I do use it. It unnerves them. They can't help watching. But it doesn't unnerve you, Mr Ferguson.'

'Not much does these days.'

'Really. Judge Curran's wife unnerved you well enough. All this talk about Thomas Cutbush.'

'Who do you think killed Patricia, Chief Inspector?'

'I think Iain Hay Gordon killed her. That's why I secured his conviction.'

'He was released, you know that? Told to take up a false identity and given a job. They knew he was stitched up.'

'Gordon repeated his confession to his first legal team. That's why they came off the record and refused to represent him. Once he confessed they couldn't represent him any more.'

'That's bar library gossip, Chief Inspector. The lawyers muddying the waters to make up for their own shortcomings.'

'Is it? Who do you think killed Patricia? I hear you had more of an interest in her than most.'

'I don't like your tone, Chief Inspector.'

'And I don't like some judge's fixer coming into my office and telling me I fitted up that little fairy for a crime he didn't commit.'

'You have to admit, if you hadn't had a confession you wouldn't have had a conviction.'

'No?'

'Patricia's body was left beside the drive. Her art folder and hat weren't there when she was found. The following morning they were there. And they were bone dry even though it had been raining all night. She'd been stabbed thirty-seven times but there was no blood on the ground around her.'

'And Judge Curran and Desmond put her body into the car and took it to the doctor's when they should have known full well she was dead, stiff as a board and cold as the grave.'

'Yes.'

'And the telephone calls, Ferguson. Are you not going to tell me about the calls? Judge Curran telephoned Patricia's friend John Steel to ask if he had seen her, fifteen minutes after the body had been found. Why would his nibs do something like that?'

'The timing of the calls was disputed.'

'The Steels were adamant at trial that they were correct. Swore blind.'

'There's no way of proving it.'

'That's the thing that troubles you, Ferguson, isn't it? Not the fact that your boss might have been involved, but that he didn't bring you into his confidence, that he kept you out in the cold?'

'Judge Curran kept everyone out in the cold, Chief Inspector, that's the kind of man he is.'

'You said there's no way of proving that Curran made that call to Steel.'

'That's right, the phone records disappeared.'

'What if someone had seen them before they disappeared? What if they showed the records to some showboating London copper who was called in to solve the case and asked him what they should do with them?'

'You saw them?' Ferguson felt cold.

'They had the records in North Queen Street barracks. They brought me in to view them. That's what I was for, after all. To clear up the mess you people had made.'

'What did they say?'

'So tell me this, Ferguson, who do you think did it? Did the judge get fed up with his slut daughter? Did mad old Doris up and at her with a knife? Who killed the girl, Ferguson, if

Gordon didn't do it?'

'What did the phone records say?'

'They confirmed the Steels' account of what happened that night. Judge Curran called the Steel house to ask where Patricia was, fifteen minutes after he knew Patricia was dead.'

'So I'm right. Gordon was innocent.'

'Gordon had no alibi for that evening. He asked another of the airmen to cover up for him. Where's the innocence in that?'

'Where are they now, the records?'

'To my knowledge Judge Curran took them.'

'There's no reason why I should believe any of this.'

'You could ask Curran. He's in London, isn't he? Lit out for pastures new. The privy council. Left you to stew in the provinces. You could go to see him at his club. The Connaught, I believe it is. If they let you in.'

'If you recall, I came here to ask you for access to a file.'

'Thomas Cutbush? Jack the Ripper? What the hell do you think you're going to find there?'

'Do you have it?'

'It's ready for you, down in the archive. Tell me something, Harry. Are times so hard you have to ask me of all people?'

'I want to know what happened.' Capstick. Of all people.

'You're like a dog returning to its vomit. You think you can make up for what you done over the years by digging into what's past and gone?'

Ferguson stood up.

'Where is the archive?'

'In the basement. The porter will show you.' Capstick got up and walked in front of him. He opened the office door.

'You'll be seeing Doris again?'

'I'll be sure to pass on your regards.'

'Do that.' Ferguson waited. He knew what was coming next.

'How's your wife?' Ferguson could see the challenge in Capstick's eyes, the sexual insolence. Ferguson looking back to November 1952. He'd tracked Esther and Capstick to a temperance hotel in Newry. Sitting outside in the car, looking up at the bedroom windows. Had Capstick known he was there? In the middle of the night Ferguson had thought he saw someone at the window. Capstick, perhaps, the policeman recognising the car outside for what it was, hearts under surveillance in the night. Holding the curtain back to look out. *Come back to bed darling.*

From the beginning Capstick had been accompanied by reporters from the London press. An air of white mischief spreading through the case. Patricia's murder finding its way into the yellow press and true crime magazines, a backdrop of suburban goings-on, hanky-panky in the post-war boom housing and new-sprung golf clubs. Capstick moving in, brutal and predatory, identifying Esther's place in the narrative. The unfaithful wife, a gin in one hand and a Dunhill cigarette in the other, eyes aglitter.

Ferguson turned at the bottom of the staircase. Capstick stood at the top, one hand on the balustrade, unmoving, a backstreet Caesar holding sway over some empire of the dead.

*

The files were waiting for Ferguson in a caged area in the

basement. An orderly showed him in, then locked the cage from the outside.

There were three separate files, the manila card folders faded and tied together with hemp twine.

Warrant of Transfer from Her Majesty's Prison Holloway to Broadmoor Prison for the Criminally Insane

Registered Number of Criminal Lunatic X32007

The first file also contained a letter from Cutbush's solicitor protesting that 'owing to the action of the Crown in raising the issue of insanity first the case was not gone into . . .'

The second file gave the dates of his incarceration and bare details of his life.

Date when he first became a criminal lunatic *14th April 1891*

Removed from Holloway to Broadmoor *15th April 1891*

Male

Former occupation *Clerk*

Single

Religious persuasion *Church of England*

Degree of education *Well*

Temperate habits *Yes*

Give brief account of the crime by which he became a criminal lunatic. *He was charged with maliciously wounding two persons by stabbing.*

Supposed cause of insanity. *Hereditary and Over Study*

How long insane. *Since 1889 at least.*

Is he known to have any previous attacks and if so when. *No record of previous attack.*

It is recorded that on 5th July 1903 his bodily health was bad. Suffered from kidney disease.

Medical condition *Demented*

Demented. Ferguson opened the second and third files and spread the foolscap pages on the desk. The pages brittle in places, rustmarks showing where they had been held together with wire paperclips. You wondered whose hand had transcribed the words, the whorled script, blotted, cursive. He lifted a sheaf of pages which appeared to be an attending physician's report, although there was no name on the pages.

Notes after Admission

A man of average height and slight build, expression vacant, eyeballs protruding. Is restless, and incoherent in conversation. Stated this morning that he had often been drunk though not a 'drinker', afterwards that he had never been drunk through drink as he had been a total abstainer for years. That the charges brought against him were absolutely false and that he had no recollection of doing anything to cause such charges to be brought against him.

That he suffered from palpitation of the heart some time ago but not lately. States he was at Peckham House Asylum 'on a visit' for a few days after he was charged with his crime. He states that there is no insanity in his family although he thinks both his mother and aunt are "bad enough" to want care in the way of being eccentric. Says he has often suffered from fits of uncontrollable temper.

20th May 1891 Struck another patient (Gilbert Cooper) suddenly and without cause whilst in the gallery.

24th August 1891 . . . well conducted lately but requires careful supervision. No improvement mentally.

16th March 1892 Violent and very destructive at times.

15th April 1893 . . . scarcely ever speaks to anyone with the exception of the principal attendant. Refuses to see any of his relations when visited by them.

22nd April 1894 Stubborn, unoccupied and silent. Makes grimaces and attitudinises when addressed.

There were no notes for the following nine years. Cutbush descending into silence. *Dark blue. Very sharp.* A final report from 20th April 1903:

Mrs Cutbush and her sister visited T. Cutbush from 2.35 to 2.55 p.m. Mrs Cutbush tried to kiss her son and he tried to bite her face then commenced to swear at them.

Died 5th January 1906.

The orderly opened the cage. Ferguson looked at his watch. Eight o'clock.

'Got to lock up now, sir. Inspector Capstick says you can take the files up to his office.

Capstick was gone, his hat and coat missing from the stand. Ferguson turned on the desk light and read on into the dark.

Rain spattered against the window. The lore of the Ripper. Seeping into the age. A London of gaslights, swirling fog. You couldn't help being drawn into it. Eleven possible Ripper victims with the five middle dead being assumed to be connected, these known as the canonical five. The other six loosely connected, the killer's method different. Dark fancies stirring in his own mind. Witnesses saw two witnesses with a 'fair-haired man'. He was later described as being 'shabby, genteel'. Capstick had included witness statements, coroners' reports. Ferguson scanning the detail of each murder, the dread methodology. The canonical five were distinguished by the fact that their throats had been cut, internal organs removed, progressive facial mutilation. He read the coroners' reports on the four later victims. It was impossible to say if they were linked. He went back to the first two. Emma Smith attacked and sexually assaulted on 3rd April 1888 and died the following day. The contemporary file reported it as a gang crime and Ferguson thought that was correct. He'd seen enough street fights in his time, the havoc of collectives.

The victim immediately before the canonical five was Martha Tabram, killed on 7th August 1888, twenty-four days before the first of the canonical five, Mary Ann Nichols. She was a prostitute and a drunkard. She'd last been seen by another prostitute, Mary Ann Connolly, also known as Pearly Poll, with an unidentified client. They parted company at 11.45 p.m. close to George Yard Buildings, an alley between Wentworth Street and Whitechapel High Street, the myth of the Ripper story beginning to close around her, the narrative murk. Pearly Poll brought her client to Angel alley. At some time before two o'clock in the morning cries of 'Murder' were heard in the area, but no attention was paid. At two Joseph and Elizabeth Mahoney returned home, climbing the stairs of George's Yard Buildings, and saw nothing. At three o'clock Albert Crow, a cab driver, saw someone lying on one of the landings but passed on. Labourer John Reeves saw the body of Martha Tabram at five in the morning and realised she was dead.

Ferguson took the autopsy report from the file. The autopsy had been carried out by the assistant pathologist for South East Middlesex, George Collier, at the Working Lads' Institute in Whitechapel. Martha Tabram had been wearing a long black jacket, a dark green skirt, a brown petticoat and stockings. She was five feet three inches tall and had dark hair.

She had been stabbed thirty-nine times.

Ferguson put the file down on the desk. He noticed that his hand was shaking a little. He wondered if death would be like this. Presences crowding the room, whispering.

Patricia Curran stabbed thirty-seven times. Martha Tabram stabbed thirty-nine times. The occult numbers. You felt there was meaning there, just out of reach. Lately Esther had begun to go to crank healers and fortune tellers. Ferguson told her that she was wasting her money and she shrugged. Now he felt he'd wandered into their territory, the numerologists and astrologers bent over their instruments in cold sitting rooms.

'You look like you seen a ghost.' Capstick was standing in the doorway. He had a bottle of Johnnie Walker and two glasses.

'Come in.'

Capstick closed the door behind him and put the bottle on the table.

'Once I get here it's hard to go home. Once a copper, always a copper. I saw your light. Did you find anything useful?'

Ferguson pushed his notebook across the desk. He had ringed the number of stab wounds in the Martha Tabram case and the Patricia Curran case. Capstick scanned it and put it back on the desk.

'What are you playing at with this Ripper stuff?'

'Doris.'

'Her own daughter?'

'If Doris thought that was who she was. If Doris was suffering from delusions.'

'Let's assume for the moment that Gordon didn't kill Patricia. What do you have? Patricia didn't get on with her mother. I heard that.'

'They talk about Patricia taking a job driving a builder's lorry. Doris hated that.'

'Thirty-seven stab wounds. Not enough.'

'It's what it shows about the Currans.' Capstick nodded. People were laid waste in the badlands of family. The nameless tracts.

'What else do we know about Patricia and the mother?'

'Only the scuttlebutt. That they didn't get on. That a large bloodstain was found in Patricia's room after the trial. Patricia's room was redecorated a week after the murder and everything in it burned.'

'And the mother was sent to the floating hotel straight after.'

'Where she remains to this day.'

'Any other physical evidence?'

'Her books and hat.'

'The Curran girl was found in the trees beside the driveway to the house.'

'There were people tramping through it all night. Police searches.'

'Very scientific, I'm sure.'

'If they'd set out to destroy the crime scene they couldn't have done more.'

'But the books and hat weren't spotted.'

'They were found the next morning. The books and hat were bone dry even though it had rained all night.'

'So someone put them there that morning.' Capstick got up and walked to the window. 'A yellow Juliet cap,' he said, his back to Ferguson, 'and five books tied together with a cord.'

Ferguson looked at the man's back. During the original investigation Capstick had discounted the presence of the Juliet cap and books. The outcome of the investigation had been predetermined, Capstick's brief to redirect suspicion away from the Curran family. This was a different man. This was the archetypal detective, lone and hampered. Capstick turned away from the window. The wind whipped the tree branches outside and light passed and repassed across the fleshy and shadowed contour of his face, the eyes dark as though they weighed the moral substance of the man he beheld.

'The blood,' Capstick said.

'What do you mean?'

'There was no blood at the scene. The girl was stabbed thirty-seven times. She would have bled like a stuck pig. Even with the rain the place would have been saturated. Once I'd seen your crime scene and not a drop there, I knew that somebody was lying through their teeth.'

Capstick walked to a wall cabinet and unlocked it with a key from his fob. He took out a legal pad and put it on the desk.

'Let's do the timing. Chummy always falls down on the timing.' He took a fountain pen from his pocket. His handwriting was small and meticulous. Patricia's last hours graven on the page.

'Patricia played squash with John Steel. She went to the bus station to take the bus to Whiteabbey.'

'The five o'clock bus.'

'We'll come back to that. She got off the bus at the Glen.'

'According to the Currans they missed her when she didn't turn up at the house. Desmond and Judge Curran started to search. Desmond found the body at 1.50 a.m.'

'He thought she was still alive. He said that she made a noise when he lifted her.'

'The lifting expels air from the lungs. It can happen. And here's the detail. Fifteen minutes later Curran calls the Steels and asks if they've seen Patricia.'

'I'm impressed, Chief Inspector.'

'Why?'

'You remember the sequence of events. The times.'

'I never forget the detail. But I've been turning this one over in my head since the day and hour.'

'Pity you didn't turn it over more at the time.'

'Hark at you, Ferguson. You and your kind ran a dirty shop from the minute you got your hands on it. You think there would have been any need for me if any of you had been straight? I cleaned up your mess for you and you'd do well to remember that.'

Ferguson stared at Capstick's writing.

'I've seen all this before. There's nothing new here, Chief Inspector.'

'That's what you think. In a proper investigation the house would have been searched and the family questioned, including Doris.'

'Judge Curran forbade it.'

'And you sat back and let him. Then you give me grief for coming in when the trail was cold. Look at this, Ferguson.' Capstick stabbed the map with his forefinger. 'The start of the journey from the bus station and the end. Nobody fucking looked hard enough at them.'

'What do you mean?'

'I sent my sergeant into the bus station. He pumped the stationmaster. The clock at the station was broken. Stuck at five o'clock. It was the ten past five bus that Patricia took home.'

'What difference does it make?'

'I'll tell you the difference it makes. Judge Curran told Steel that Patricia had taken the five o'clock bus home. Only one person could have told Curran what bus she took home and mistaken the time.'

'Patricia.'

'Now you're getting it.'

'The other thing you found out. What is it?'

'It ties in. I want you to tell me what the gates to the Glen looked like.'

Ferguson leaned back in his chair and shut his eyes. There were two limestone pillars to either side of the entrance, the barrel of the pillar fluted with a domed capstone. To the right of the entrance stood the single-storey gatehouse. There was a bus stop to the left of the entrance and a low sea wall on the other side of the road. The driveway was enclosed on one side by iron railings and on the other by trees. It rose away from the road, curving to the right, then sharply angled to the left. It was at the apex of the angle that Patricia's body was found, dragged into the trees.

Esther had never liked driving to the Glen at night. She said afterwards that the driveway felt like one of the places that might draw crime to itself. The moorland settings and lonely riverbanks, all the death-haunted locales. She read true crime magazines. She was an aficionado of sprawled corpses, crime-scene vernaculars, eyes open and staring, lipstick awry.

'Did you notice the phone box?' Capstick said.

'Was there one?'

'At the bus stop. See, I was thinking, it's a lonely walk for a young girl in the dark, so I do a bit of asking and Mrs McCrink, the housekeeper, she tells me that Patricia never walks up the drive. She always telephones the house and someone comes down for her in a car.'

'You think Patricia didn't walk up the drive?'

'It wasn't her habit.'

'She could have called and found there was no one there, then decided to walk.'

'Doris was in the house until seven thirty. I don't know about any of the rest of them.'

'Doris couldn't have done it, Chief Inspector, not to her own daughter.'

'Anyone is capable of anything, Mr Ferguson. Flesh and blood's no bar to murder. People kill for greed or a grope.'

'Patricia was stabbed twenty-one times in the chest. Thirty-seven in all.' The knife rising and falling. The killer gore-drenched.

'It doesn't signify. People save their worst for them that's closest.'

'The physical strength required. It doesn't seem likely

from a woman.'

'When it comes to the shedding of blood, a woman can do anything a man can. A woman's hand wrote the book on harm, Mr Ferguson.'

'Cutbush.'

'What brings you to him?'

'Doris said his name. She was at Broadmoor at the same time.'

'So there was a dead lunatic lurking in the shrubbery?'

'That's not what I mean.'

'What do you mean then?' But Ferguson did not answer. Cutbush's eyes on him, summoned from out of the night.

Thirteen

28TH JULY 1949

Ferguson took his seat in the public gallery. He could see Taylor shifting in his seat, rubbing his thumbnail along the edge of the dock, testing the varnish, warmed and softened by the sun although it was only ten thirty.

Lily sat to one side, still wearing her widow's garb, her hands folded in her lap. Lunn had told her to sit like that, the fabric smoothed taut over her belly so that the jury and public could see that she was pregnant.

Patricia sat down beside Ferguson. She was wearing a long gaberdine coat.

'It's warm in here,' Ferguson said, 'you won't last the morning.'

'Can't take it off,' Patricia said, 'I've got my hockey skirt on underneath. I'm playing at lunchtime. His honour would have kittens. Besides, if Father can make it through wearing a gown and wig, I can make it in a raincoat.'

'You look like one of those men in the bushes at the park,' Hilary had said.

'Maybe I should flash Harry,' Patricia said.

'Don't be awful, Patricia. Besides, I think Mrs Ferguson might have a thing or two to say about it.'

'I heard Mother's bridge ladies talking about her,' Patricia said. 'They seem to think she's a bit fast, Harry or no Harry. Why are you looking at me like that?

'Because I talk about doing things but never do them, Patricia. I'm all talk. But you just go ahead and do things.'

'What? Like flash Harry Ferguson?'

'That's not what I meant.'

'Don't turn all grim on me, Hilary. You'll give yourself lines. A crone before your time.'

The judge instructed defence counsel to address the jury. Hanna began his summation at ten thirty-five. Mary McGowan was confused. The blood on Taylor's trousers was in fact paint. Mary McGowan's senses were disordered by the blows to her head. She had named Taylor but she was mistaken. The motive did not exist, for no one would kill for such a small sum of money.

'I'm almost starting to feel sorry for Taylor,' Patricia said. 'He's not much older than I am.'

'Don't,' Ferguson said. He could see that Taylor wasn't looking at his counsel. He had noticed Patricia in the body of the court and his eyes were drawn to her. Later that morning Patricia became aware of his eyes. It made her nervous, she told Hilary afterwards. It was as if Taylor knew why she was wearing the trenchcoat and what she was wearing underneath it.

'He has these button eyes and freckles. The way he was looking at me gave me the creeps, Hilary. It was like hands on you.'

Patricia found herself moving closer to Ferguson. Taylor seemed to notice the movement. She thought she saw him smiling at her.

Hanna's summing up took an hour and forty-five minutes.

The court adjourned for lunch. Patricia followed Ferguson out into the hallway. He saw Esther coming towards him.

'Go and get yourself something to eat,' Ferguson said. 'I've got something to do.'

'I thought we'd talk about the case,' Patricia said.

'Go,' Ferguson said. He crossed the foyer to meet Esther. 'I've got to get to McKenzie before Curran sums up.'

'Who's McKenzie?'

'The foreman of the jury.'

'I thought you'd got to the jury.'

'The courtroom's a place where things are bought and sold, same as anything else, and I'm the broker. There's still work to be done.'

'That poor woman's life has a price.'

'I made a bargain with McKenzie and I need to make sure he keeps it.'

'How do you know he won't?'

'Because Hanna has no case. And your father is about to tear Taylor to shreds in there and send him out of this courthouse with a noose around his neck.'

Ferguson walked down the corridor to the doorway which led to the rear of the jury room. He looked over his shoulder. Patricia was standing where he had left her, holding the gabardine closed at her throat with one hand as though she was chilled.

The policeman at the door stood aside. Ferguson nodded to him. The corridor beyond the door was quiet and still. The jury room was at the end of the corridor. There was a gents' toilet halfway along with an alcove opposite. Ferguson stood in the alcove. One of the jurors left the jury room and went into the toilet without seeing him, a small bald man with the look of a small-town shopkeeper, used to weighing out of dry goods, totting sums on the back of brown paper bags. Ferguson waited for him to leave the toilet. No air moved in the enclosed corridor and he felt sweat on his back. The jury room door opened. McKenzie. Ferguson waited for him to pass the alcove, then put a hand in his back and pushed him through the toilet door. He turned McKenzie and backed him up against the sinks.

'What do you want from me, Ferguson? The man's as guilty as sin. A child could see it.'

'I don't care what a child can see. How many?'

'How many what?'

'How many calls for a guilty verdict?'

'Unanimous.'

Ferguson moved closer to McKenzie. He could see his face reflected in the flyspecked mirror over the man's shoulder. He looked detached. A scholar in the sciences of harm. He could hear water flushing behind him.

'Do you know what this place reminds me of?'

'What?'

'The morgue. The autopsy room. Where they slice the bodies.' He could see the fear in McKenzie's face. 'The last time I was in there was after the riots in '42. There were seven bodies on trolleys ready for the knife. I don't want to see that tomorrow morning, McKenzie. You go back in there and tell them you're voting not guilty.'

'I already told them yes.'

'You changed your mind. You had a conversion in here. The angel of the Lord came unto you.'

'They won't swallow that.'

'I don't care what they swallow. Your customers find out that you sent Taylor to the hangman, you're done, McKenzie. You can shut up shop tomorrow.'

'I'll do it.'

'You better.'

Ferguson released McKenzie. He could still see his own face in the mirror. Judgement hanging in the glass. He walked away from McKenzie, his heels clicking on the tiled floor. In the corridor he stopped and leaned against the wall. The jury room was to his left. Dust motes in the air. A monkish calm.

Ferguson knocked on the inside of the door from the jury quarters. The policeman opened it and stood back to let Ferguson out. Curran was passing on the other side of the hallway. He looked up from the affidavit in his hand and saw Ferguson come out. Curran stopped. He knew there was only one reason for Ferguson to be in the jury quarters.

'Do you think I will not adequately convince them, Ferguson?'

'I was just using the bathroom, Mr Curran.' Curran looked down at the paper in his hand as though it might address a query as to his own substance, what character of man he was, what defect?

'I was using the bathroom, Mr Curran.' Curran shook his head and walked on. Ferguson felt Patricia's hand on his arm.

'I ducked into the foyer when I saw Father,' she said. 'He'd go spare if he saw me in this old coat.'

'I thought you had hockey?'

'I didn't want to miss the exciting denouement. The miscreant sent to the hangman's embrace.'

'It's not funny,' Ferguson said, 'even for someone like Taylor.'

'I'm sorry. It isn't funny. There's a bloodthirsty part of me wants someone to pay for that poor little lady.'

'He told you off,' Hilary said afterwards. 'How very stern and manly. Was it very thrilling, Patricia?'

'That part of it was. The rest of it wasn't any fun though.'

'Was your father not utterly devastating?'

'He was. He was cold like ice. '

The court resumed at two o'clock. Curran's address to the jury lasted for one hour. He pointed out that the victim, Mary McGowan, had identified Taylor on four separate occasions to different witnesses. Hanna had argued that Mrs McGowan had been confused and mistaken following blows to the head. But Curran said that on the morning of the murder the victim had in fact opened the door to Taylor when he asked to use the telephone precisely because she knew him and this was before the blows to the head had been struck.

Taylor looked at Hanna but the counsel did not return the look.

'Old Hanna didn't see that one coming, did he?' Patricia said. Her eyes were bright.

'You're not at the pictures,' Ferguson said.

As to the imputation that there was some motive of revenge in Mrs McGowan's identification of Taylor, there was no reason for vengeance as Taylor had never previously wronged Mrs McGowan.

Curran turned to the direct evidence against Taylor. He had lied to the police about his proximity to the crime. There were fibres from the victim's clothing on his clothes. There were hairs which matched the victim's. There was cereal which matched the cereal in the soup which had been poured over the victim. There was blood on his shoes. There was blood on his coat, on his shirt, jacket, trousers and socks. He had claimed the blood was paint, knowing it was not so. He had then told the police that the blood had come from massive nosebleeds which he had neglected to mention during interrogation.

Curran left the question of motive until last. He spoke of 'poor Miss Jones' and Taylor's need for money in order to proceed with the marriage which had been planned for two days after the murder of Mary McGowan.

'I need not make the case against the accused,' Curran said. 'The examinations have made the case themselves. The jury must look at the facts laid in front of them. They must not let the consequences of their verdict sway them. Their duty is clear.'

When he had finished Lily turned her head to look at Curran, her face invisible beneath the black veil. She moved her head as though a figure of death acknowledged its familiar. Taylor smoothed his hair back nervously. Judge Shiel announced a brief recess and the court rose.

'Your father was inch-perfect,' Ferguson said. 'He let the facts speak for themselves. No more and no less. No fancy stuff.'

'A little bit of fancy stuff,' Patricia said. 'The way he said that Mrs McGowan opened the door to Taylor before the blows to the head so that she must have known him.'

'Fair enough. What else?'

'The end of his speech. Saying that the defence brought about their own downfall by introducing evidence in cross-examination.'

'You think that was clever?'

'I think it was true. We all bring about our own downfall, whether we mean to or not, don't we, Harry?'

She brushed against him and began to walk towards the court exit.

'Where are you going?' Ferguson said.

'Hockey,' she said, 'remember?' She turned back towards him and with a quick glance around, opened her coat to the blouse and hockey skirt underneath.

The court returned at three thirty. The judge's address to the jury lasted for three hours. Breaking down the case for them, explaining the law, surrounding the events of the day of the murder with moment and gravity. A handbag open on a kitchen table, an earring lying in a clot of blood on the floor. It was important to bring understanding to these things. A girl in black in the body of the court. If the law was for nothing else it was to give shape and weight to the everyday when things were thrown off course. The judge looked over his glasses at the twelve members of the jury. They must act in earnest. They were ratepayers, holders of premises and of offices, and must use the gravity of their position to anchor the world for all. It was a fair summing up, Ferguson thought. Shiel knew what he was up against and had held the line. He stared at McKenzie throughout but McKenzie wouldn't meet his eye. Hanna and Lunn conferred together. Taylor looked around the courtroom but none met his gaze. He rubbed his arms and pinched the flesh on the inside of his wrists. Ferguson saw him rub his neck. *Well may you touch that young neck,* Ferguson thought, *for if McKenzie fails me, it'll feel the bite of the hemp, the pinch of it.*

As Judge Shiel drew to a close Ferguson looked up and saw the curator Harvey enter the court and take a seat opposite. Curran glanced upwards towards Harvey. All was in place now. All was in play. Curran folded his hands in his lap and waited for the judge to rise. When he was gone and the jury had filed back into their room, Hanna and Lunn hurried from the courtroom. The public gallery emptied. Lily did not move, nor did Curran. Harvey got to his feet but did not leave.

Outside the court precincts had filled with the news that the jury had retired, the people close-packed. Harvey crossed the courtroom to join Ferguson, leaving the body of the room empty save for Lily and Curran, the silent, veiled girl and the Attorney General in wig and frock coat. They faced each other across the courtroom like silent duellists. In the court yards the crowd grew in number, spilling out in the streets, massing against the walls of the building.

'The Special Constabulary have been called up,' Harvey said.

'They're as likely to lead the mob,' Ferguson said. There were sunspots on the backs of Harvey's hands. He brought an air of dusty colonial squares to the courtroom, the muezzin's call, the sound of distant pogrom. An hour passed. There were murmurs from the crowd outside. The murmurs subsided, but Ferguson heard scurrying feet through the open courtroom window.

'Will the court rise for the night?' Harvey asked.

'No. This will have to be finished,' Ferguson said.

'What's wrong with Curran?'

'He expected the jury to come straight back in. He didn't think there would be any debate about the verdict.'

'And you?'

'I have faith in our system of justice.'

Eight thirty. The scurrying outside the window had turned to shuffling. Ferguson could hear the engines of police tenders on Chichester Street. He looked at the door of the jury room. He thought about McKenzie backed into a corner. *Stand your ground, man.*

At nine thirty a police sergeant conveyed a note from the jury to the court clerk. They were ready to return. Curran did not lift his head as the public re-entered. Taylor entered with a gaoler to each side. One of the wardens guided Taylor towards the box when it looked as though he might keep on going into the body of the courtroom, break into a stumbling run.

A tipstaff came from the judge's quarters. He was carrying a square of black silk and he placed it to the right of the judge's seat that it might be to hand. The junior counsel and clerks took their places in the body of the court. The jury filed into their box. McKenzie would not meet Ferguson's eyes. His face was red and he kept his gaze fixed on the floor in front of him. Taylor's eyes kept going to the square of silk on the bench, his fingers moving. If he could handle the black material he would know its properties. The tipstaff stood to announce the judge's entry. As he did so the court door opened and Lily entered, still attired in black and veiled. As the court rose for the judge she crossed the perimeter to her place in the gallery. Judge Shiel crossed the dais between his quarters and the bench and it seemed he changed places with Lily in some strange gavotte.

As the court took their seats Ferguson felt Patricia push into the seat beside him.

'He doesn't look so cocky now, does he?' she said. Taylor was holding the stanchions of the dock tightly. His cheek twitched. Ferguson thought that he might start to weep like a child, great racking sobs, his shoulders heaving.

'He'll cry like a baby if it goes against him,' Patricia said, 'snot everywhere.'

'Has the jury reached a verdict?' Shiel asked. McKenzie got to his feet, his eyes downcast. He said something. The court craned forward to hear his words.

'Speak up please, Mr Foreman,' the judge said. As he leaned forward his sleeve brushed the silk square and he looked down at it.

'We are unable to reach a verdict, your honour,' McKenzie said.

'I see,' Shiel said. 'As I have told you, I must have a unanimous verdict in this case. If the jury is returned to its deliberations, given more time, are they likely to overcome their differences?'

'No, your honour,' McKenzie said, 'their minds are dead set, one way or the other. There's no shifting them.'

'Are you sure, Mr Foreman?'

'Nothing more certain on God's earth.'

'In that case it is my duty to declare a mistrial and to thank the gentlemen of the jury for their service. The defendant is free to go.'

Fourteen

MARCH 1961

Doris would say to her children that the days of her childhood in Broadmoor were the happiest of her life. Desmond looked at her sideways when she said it but Patricia was always at her for details. Tell me about the skull on Grandpa's desk. Tell me about the madwomen and their bare feet and their frizzy hair and about the pale-faced murderers alone in their cells. Tell me about the howling at night.

When she was small Patricia would tell adults that Mother always liked being behind bars and then she'd give Doris what she called her secret smile. She'd tell them Mummy was brought up in the mental which put Doris's teeth on edge. The Malone Road ladies and the Whiteabbey ladies all thought they were superior but Harry Ferguson said, 'Don't mind them, Mrs Curran, that's what happens when you live in the provinces, you become a snob.' She told Desmond that Ferguson was nice and spoke well to her, but Desmond said, 'For God's sake, Mother, Ferguson is Father's fixer. You don't think Father gets elected because the people love him, do you?'

Still Ferguson had a sadness about him that no one could see but she, and it could not be gainsaid. She had her own secret sorrow which many had tried to find but none could know.

The psychiatrist, Mr Brown, spoke to her three times a week

at the start but now she hardly ever saw him. He wore a tweed jacket and tie and had a line of pens in his top pocket. You were supposed to think that he had walked in the lonely halls of the mind but he did not fool Doris for one minute. Those who had been in the halls of the mind were not kindly. They did not nod in understanding. They did not carry a line of pens in their pocket. They were ice. He wanted her to name them but she would not. They were the unnamed.

When she said that she did not know what Mr Brown was talking about she could feel Lucy smile. And sometimes she felt Cutbush smile from the shadows.

Mr Brown prescribed Largactil for her. The nurses would give her the tablets with a glass of water and wait for her to swallow them. Lucy had shown her all the tricks the patients used in Broadmoor. To hide the tablets under your tongue or to drop them into your lap and sweep the folds of your skirt over them. Lucy had showed her how to search a skirt and how to hold a patient's nose to make them swallow. They don't like their dose, Lucy said, but they have to take it otherwise they'll be raving and there'll be no peace in this place.

Mr Brown kept trying to bring her back to the night of 12th November 1952. That was the way he spoke. *The night of 12th November 1952.* As if he was a policeman like Mr Capstick, so that Doris had to tell him that Lady Curran would not be subject to questioning like a common criminal.

'Of course, Lady Curran,' he answered her. *Lady Curran Lady Muck* was what Lucy would have said to that. *My sweet arse* she would have said.

'What happened that night, do you remember?' Mr Brown asked again and again.

'I want to talk about the night of the twenty-eighth of July 1949,' Doris told him.

'Why that night, Mrs Curran?'

'That was the end of the first Taylor trial.'

'The Taylor trial?'

'Robert Taylor was charged with the murder of a Roman Catholic woman. My husband, the Attorney General, prosecuted.'

'Of course. Why does that night stand out in your mind?'

'It was the night the case finished. My husband had a disagreement with Harry Ferguson.'

'Mr Ferguson. His election agent.'

'Harry wanted him to stop.'

'I don't understand.'

'The jury in the Taylor case did not reach a verdict. The decision fell to my husband as Attorney General.'

Doris had awakened to the sound of voices in the drawing room. She put on her dressing gown and went down the stairs to the drawing-room door. She thought to knock but did not. Ferguson sounded like a man who was angry but wished not to show it. Her husband sounded like the winter.

'You played the hand that was given you as best you could. You cut Taylor to pieces in the witness box. Everybody seen what you done with the case. Now let sleeping dogs lie, Mr Curran. There's no winning this case.'

'I intend to press for a retrial.'

'You'll only get the same result or worse.'

'Look.' Doris could hear the floorboards creak as Ferguson crossed them and she feared that he would catch her at the door. But she heard the curtains being opened. 'It's quiet out there tonight. There's no sirens. There's no houses burned. There won't be a queue out the door of the coroner's court in the morning. We won. Everybody knows what Taylor done. He'll get his comeuppance somewhere along the line. People get what they deserve.'

'Will you get what you deserve out of this affair, Harry? Will I?'

'You'll get a seat on the bench, if it wasn't yours already.'

'And you?'

'A rising tide lifts many a boat.'

'And yet you hazarded more than I did in the case.'

'Did I?'

'You forget I saw you emerge from the jury room. McKenzie?'

'The jury reached its own verdict.'

'Perhaps a verdict it might have reached anyway, however unjust. But you made certain.'

'What's done is done. The woman's dead and there's no bringing her back.'

'Retribution will be exacted.'

'If you go back to the well on this and win then you might as well kiss that ermine collar goodbye.'

'Then let us set out a forfeit in the open this time, Harry. I will undertake to win the case. You may undertake to prevent my winning.'

'You're making a game out of it.'

'Everything we undertake is a game.'

'If I win?'

'Then I will follow your advice in all things. I will act according to self-interest.'

'And if I lose?'

'That seems clear enough, Harry. If I carry the day, then you lose your job, and I lose mine.'

'It seems as fair as anything in this life. You can convince the cabinet and the DPP to go after Taylor again?'

'They will do my bidding on pain of my resignation. Have Taylor rearrested, Harry.'

'It's already done.'

'He is in custody?'

'I had him lifted this evening. He's now residing in a cell in Crumlin Road. You're not the only person round here can read a man's heart, Mr Curran.'

'Your office is very untidy, Mr Brown.'

'Is it important to you that things are tidy, Mrs Curran?'

'No more than anyone else,' Doris said. Lucy used to say that the bigshot doctors came into Broadmoor with grave looks but that when they went home it was the likes of her that had to deal with the patients when they went off the deep end, not Mr Learned Title.

Lucy could not remember people's proper names so she gave them nicknames, a habit that Doris found herself adopting in the hospital.

It was all Broadmoor then with Mr Brown. Did you have access to the hospital building? Did you have any communication with any of the patients? Were your parents always there and did you get on with them? Did you ever find yourself alone with any of the patients? Every time he asked a question he gave that laugh again. It was a laugh such as someone makes when they want you to think they are apologising but they are not sorry.

She didn't like the way he acted, like he was her friend, and saying that he'd soon have her back on her feet. My feet are not the problem, she wanted to say, this is not a hospital for feet.

He asked if she considered her childhood to be a happy one and she said it was as happy as anyone else's but she did not say that you did not talk about happiness or even think about it in Broadmoor. He wanted to know if she had many friends when she was small. She said that she had lots of friends but that was a lie. Two could play at that game. At school they called her mad Doris because she lived at the asylum. The smell of it was about her person.

Did you ever bring friends home, he asked her. Their parents would not allow it, she said. They imagined child abductors roaming the grounds of Broadmoor, slack-mouthed men with pale skins padding in the corridors. Go home with mad Doris? they said, not bloody likely.

What did you feel about that? Brown said. She shrugged. When she was small Lucy had asked her the same question and when she told her, Lucy said never you mind them nasty little misses. If Lucy got a hold of them she would give them what for.

So you were very lonely growing up was what he came out with next. I was friends with some of the staff, Doris replied. Who was that? he asked quick as a flash, no apologetic laugh this time, but Doris was ready for him. Oh, just one of the kitchen girls, Doris said, I can't even remember her name now. Good girl, Lucy whispered, that put a stop to Mr Brown's gallop and no mistake.

After that they talked about whether she was depressed or sad when her children were born and Doris said she wasn't, she didn't have time to be depressed in London where Patricia was born. Curran had insisted that she go to a public hospital. Brown was interested in that, so Doris told him about the ward with plaster falling from the walls and the East End girls groaning and swearing in the most appalling way.

Mr Brown put the top on his pen and said that will be all for today, Mrs Curran. He got up and opened the office door for her. Oh by the way, he said as she was walking through, with a big innocent face like she wouldn't notice what he was at, what did you say the name of the kitchen girl at Broadmoor was? I told you I don't remember, Doris said, pert as you like, and she kept walking.

That's my girl, Lucy said. *That's my lass.*

Fifteen

JANUARY 1961

Ferguson woke early. He went down to the kitchen in the dark. He made no noise in passing Esther's room. As he poured hot water from the kettle he looked up and saw her framed in the doorway.

'Nine years ago you were standing in the same place. It was dark then as well.'

'Was it?'

'You were still wearing your overcoat. There was mud on your shoes. You told me that you had just come from Judge Curran's house. That something dreadful had happened. Patricia had been found murdered.'

'Yes. I remember.'

'Your hand was shaking so much you could barely hold the kettle. It was dark and I couldn't see your eyes.'

'Nine years. It feels like longer.'

'You need to talk to Gordon. To that policeman, Capstick.'

'Gordon was convicted of the murder.'

'But you don't think he did it. You know he didn't do it.'

'So what's the point of talking to him?'

'You need to find out who killed her, Harry. Do it for yourself or do it for her. It makes no difference.'

'I'll talk to Gordon again.'

'He didn't kill Patricia. They put him in the asylum for nothing.'

'I want to hear what he has to say.'

'Him in the same place as Doris Curran. I wonder does he know?'

'I wonder does she know?'

It was still dark when Ferguson got to his car. It had rained without cease until morning on the night that Patricia had died. This morning there was frost on the windscreen. He scraped it off with his hand and got into the car. Sleet struck the bodywork. It grew light. He drove along the lough. At Whiteabbey he pulled the car on to the pavement opposite the entrance to the Glen. There were lines of sleet coming in across the channel and out beyond the channel markers the tidal race drove spume across the sandbars and foul ground at the Mew Island light.

He crossed the road to the phone box at the gates and rang Holywell Mental Hospital. He made an appointment with the superintendent. As he replaced the receiver a Lancia drove out of the entrance to the Glen. He saw Lance Curran in profile, the thin mouth downturned, the gloved hands on the wheel. Ferguson remembered the night of Patricia's death. Her body had been placed in the back seat of the car. Rigor mortis had set in, although Desmond Curran had claimed that he had heard Patricia breathing. The stiff body would not fit into the car and her legs protruded from the open window. They had driven down the avenue in convoy. Ferguson wondered if Curran thought of it as he left for court in the morning. His daughter's body in the back seat of a car like some doleful mannikin.

Where was the blood? he thought. Stabbed thirty-seven times. There must have been blood in the car and on their clothing but Ferguson had seen none when he came to the scene in the early morning.

Curran glanced at the phone box but the windows were fogged and he could not have seen Ferguson. He pulled into the sparse early morning traffic. A wave broke on the sea wall and spray covered the car. The wind blew the spray down the road against the windows of the phone box. When it was gone the car was no longer visible. There was always a sleight of hand at work with the Currans. Objects and people appearing and disappearing. Patricia's hat and books appeared at the edge of the trees. The telephone records from the night disappeared. Patricia dead. Gordon and Doris incarcerated. A music-hall conjuring act of drapes and levers with Curran as top-hatted master of ceremonies.

Holywell was a Victorian asylum, the main building surrounded by an ancillary complex over several acres. He drove through it for ten minutes before he reached the entrance to the secure unit, finding himself in annexes, dead ends, buildings with windows bricked up behind high walls. He kept ending up back in the same place. You thought of a still room, someone sitting on a steel-framed bed making rocking movements.

A nurse led him to the superintendent's office. The superintendent was waiting for him. He was a balding man wearing a blazer with a rowing club crest on the pocket. He stood to shake Ferguson's hand.

'You want to interview Iain Hay Gordon, Mr Ferguson?'

'That's what I came up here for.'

'I see. May I ask you the purpose of the interview?'

'I don't think that's appropriate. How has he been?'

'I have already stated my opinion that Mr Hay Gordon is as sane as you or I and should never have been committed to the care of this institution. While he was in my care he was anxious, neurotic, but not insane.'

'You say was. Past tense.'

'Iain Hay Gordon is no longer an inmate of Holywell.'

'Is that a fact? Well if he isn't an inmate of Holywell, where is he an inmate of?'

'I don't know.'

'What happened? Did he escape? Over the wall and leg it?'

'He was released by order of the Minister for Home Affairs.'

'When?'

'Two months ago.'

'Where is he now?'

'We were given no forwarding details.'

'A patient leaves a secure mental hospital with no forwarding details.'

'My information is that he was given a new identity and employment on the basis that he conceal his identity.'

'Who organised this?'

'I received a telephone call from the minister's representative.'

'So all this was done on a phone call. No paperwork.'

'I was assured it wasn't necessary.'

'You didn't tell me.'

'You didn't ask.'

Ferguson bowed his head. He detected the hand of Curran again.

'Did you ever see a magician on the stage, Mr Brown?'

'Years ago. When I was young.' You were never young,

Ferguson thought.

'I saw an act once. In the town hall in Warrenpoint. The magician got a girl to come up from the audience and step into a cabinet. She looked nervy, shook, trying to smile, looking back at her friends. The magician closed the door and when he opened it again she was gone. He closed it again, opened it, and hey presto, there she was.'

When the cabinet door opened on an empty space the theatre was silent and the magician eyed them without speaking, one black-cloaked arm extended. He offered them access to the old worlds, to whispered tales of those that were carried off never to return. The vanished and the stolen. All they had to do was follow the girl. All they had to do was step inside.

'It's not the fact that the magician makes you disappear that scares the audience,' Ferguson said, getting up. 'It's the fear that you might never come back at all.'

He walked down the corridor. Inmates stood alone in gowns and did not raise their eyes at his passing. A woman was embarked on some point of debate with herself. Ferguson scanned their faces, thinking that he might see Doris Curran and hoping that he would not. He remembered when he had last seen the Belfast Rowing Club logo. It had been on the tie worn by the museum curator Ellis Harvey the night he had walked to the museum with him from the Reform Club.

Esther was home before him. She sat on the edge of the lounge settee. She was still wearing her hat and coat, her back straight, looking poised, unnatural.

'What is it?'

'A girl was killed in Newry last night. They found her in a

field this morning.'

'I didn't hear the news.'

'She was nineteen. Same age as Patricia. The scuttlebutt is that she was found naked. There were bruises all over her. He tried to strangle her.'

'Strangled.'

'He beat her and tried to strangle her, then he stabbed her to death, Harry.'

'You seem to know a lot about it.'

'I was in the RUC club in Knockbreda this evening. It was all the talk. The Newry police know who did it.'

'That'll make a change around here.'

'They're not arresting him yet. They say they need hard evidence.'

'It's always a help. I went to Holywell today.'

'Gordon?'

'He's not there. They gave him a false name and told him to keep his mouth shut. He's in hiding somewhere. Scotland's my guess.'

'Why would they do that?'

'Gives them a hold over him. Letting him know that his freedom is in their gift. They couldn't keep him in Holywell forever with the superintendent saying that he's sane, so this is the next best thing.'

'The next best thing?'

'They would have preferred him dead but that would bring its own set of problems.'

'That poor little man locked up in the asylum for something he didn't do. Day after day. What would a person do in the asylum, Harry, when all they want to do is get out but people won't let them?'

There were days when Esther would sit at the kitchen table smoking cigarettes. She did not dress. Her hair was untended. He knew the undercurrents, the small brittle gestures, the theatre of sexual harm.

He had brought the Whiteabbey GP, Wilson, to see her. Afterwards she had berated him softly. She told him of assignations, casual encounters, her account detailed and cutting. She named men he knew. She told him how she brought out a rank carnality in them. She fell asleep afterwards. In the morning she remembered nothing. He found the empty prescription jar that Wilson had left in the bin, the capsules ground underfoot on the back step.

Wilson called him a few days later and asked him to come to the surgery. Wilson said he had obtained Esther's medical records, which indicated that she had spent some time as an in-patient of the Downshire hospital in her teens. The Downshire was a mental institution on the periphery of the city.

'How long?'

'Several months each time. They record fugue states interspersed with hysteria.'

'Hysteria?'

'That's what it says. Following unspecified trauma. She was committed by the family doctor.'

'How long did this go on for?'

'November 1947 was the last incarceration.'

Ferguson had met Esther in January 1947. He had worked in Nuremberg that year. He remembered black trees outside and snow. She had written to him to say that it was snowing there as well. She said that she had walked in the snow at dusk.

Pathos her stock in trade.

'Did she tell you about it?'

'No.' Ferguson trying to work out dates. Wondering if she had come to their encounters straight from Holywell. She would send him notes telling him where to meet her, signed and imprinted with the shape of her mouth in lipstick beside her name. She would meet him outside York Street bus station or the King's Hall and they'd drive to the hotel she had booked. She liked to sign the register as Mr and Mrs Harry Ferguson. Needing to lie about it. She liked to see herself as damaged. She would arrange the room in the manner of a married couple, hanging his shirts in the wardrobe, adopting a brittle and suburban manner. She referred to him as her husband in provincial dining rooms, insisting that he hold her chair at the table. She would talk to other couples of a future of suburban bridge games, boarding schools for children.

Looking back he could see that they engaged in a phantasm of marriage. She would come to him at night then and lay herself bare to him, hollow-eyed, ravening.

The death of the Newry girl was reported in the papers the following day. There were photographs of the crime scene, a place known as Weir's Rock. Policemen standing guard over rough terrain. The victim was a shop girl called Pearl Gamble. She had last been seen at a dance in a local Orange hall. A blurred photograph showed a girl with slant oriental eyes and a gap in her front teeth. The newpaper report said that her effects had been found scattered over the quarter-mile distance between the place where she had been dropped off by friends and Weir's Rock. A shoe, her brassiere, her blouse stained with blood.

Esther went out every night to police haunts and returned with information, wide-eyed, lost in the girl's murder, the detail of it, the forensics of the heart. She told Ferguson about the massive blood loss, the ripped nylons. The ligature marks on the girl's neck and the torn fingernails indicating she had struggled. The multiple stab wounds on neck and torso. She said that a sergeant had taken a spade and filled a bucket with earth saturated in blood. Ferguson did not ask her where she had got her information, or what bargains she had made in return for it.

'They're putting pressure on a suspect,' she said. 'They hope he'll make a slip-up.' Ferguson saw the reports in the papers the next day. A man named McGladdery, a provincial wide boy. The London newspapers in town filing copy from public phones, calling him the Pied Piper, following him around, hungry for sex crime innuendo, McGladdery revelling in the attention. Detectives outside his home, watching him from parked cars. Ten days after the murder he was arrested following the discovery of stained clothing hidden in a septic tank near his home at Damolly.

'They all say he's guilty as sin,' Esther said.

'That's no guarantee.'

'Guarantee that he'll be convicted or that he'll get off?'

'Either.'

'Do you know who the judge is? Harry? I asked you a question.' Esther was pale, her eyes fixed on Ferguson.

'I do.'

'He can't, Harry.'

'He put himself on the list for it.'

'If Curran is the judge that man will be convicted, innocent or guilty.'

'You think I don't know that?'

'The jury will take one look at him on the bench and they'll think about Patricia. McGladdery will be made to pay for Patricia's death.'

'Yes.'

'And Curran will let them do it.'

'Probably. He might even encourage them, Esther.'

'You put him on that bench, Harry. You need to fix it so that Curran doesn't try McGladdery.'

'By finding who killed Patricia. You think it's as simple as that.'

'Nothing's that simple, but you owe it to Patricia and to Doris and to that poor woman McGowan who died in 1949.'

Sixteen

Brown had wanted to know about Doris's mother but Doris said she could not tell him very much as her mother had died when she was young.

Lucy said that was a lie, you naughty thing, your mother was not dead, but Doris said so what? Brown was too nosy by half, tell him anything and he'd write it down.

She remembered that her mother was tall with bright red lipstick on a thin mouth and she wore leather gloves even when she was in the house. Father wanted her to take them off but she said that everywhere was covered in germs and bacilli and she would only take the gloves off in order to wash her hands, rinsing them under the tap again and again.

Often Mother was not there when Doris came home from school and when she asked where she was Father said that she had one of her headaches but that Lucy would look after Doris. Doris asked Lucy if headaches went on for days. They must do because her mother was often gone with them. It must be terrible, Doris said.

'There's plenty like her in this house of Broadmoor with them kind of headaches,' Lucy said.

'What's good for headaches?' Doris said.

'Damn all me or you can do to help that class of thing,' Lucy said. 'If there was flowers here it might cheer her up but there's nothing except the cold grey stone.'

There were flowers in Broadmoor. Doris was surprised that Lucy didn't seem to know. They were grown in the garden at the side of Male Medical. There were lilies and carnations which Father wore in his buttonhole and pink roses which grew on into the frost of November.

Doris went to the garden although she was not allowed. She told the warder at the door between their house and her father's office that she had been summoned to him. The man unlocked the door and told her to go to the office and not to turn aside from her path and Doris nodded her head and said yes.

Frost lay on the garden since morning as the high walls blocked sunlight on winter days. The cold frames were empty and the earth sat in frozen clods on the beds. The roses that stood against the north wall were wizened and without bloom. Doris was disappointed as there would be no flowers for her mother. She saw that there was a man standing under the eaves of the garden shed. He was still with his hands by his sides as though he stood sentry to something within. He raised one hand. She thought that his hands must be cold standing out in the frost. He unbent one of his cold hands and crooked his finger to summon her.

'What is your name?' he said. She could see little of his face in the shadow of the eaves.

'Doris.'

'What are you looking for, Doris?'

'I am looking for flowers for Mother. These ones are all dead.'

'There are flowers in the shed behind me. They keep all the best ones as their own. They can't help themselves.'

'Maybe I should go back.'

'It would be a shame to go back without flowers for your mother. They say a mother's love is a blessing.'

'What are you doing here?'

'They let me come down here for fresh air. I don't tell them I can smell the flowers that are hidden.'

'What's your name?'

'My name is Saucy Jack.' He seemed to step forward a little into the frozen winter light. She could see that his eyes were dark blue.

'I'm not supposed to be here,' she said.

'Saucy Jack never tells.'

'I'd better go back.'

'Without flowers for your mother? She might be sad.'

'Where did you get the flowers?' Lucy said.

'They're for Mother.'

'I didn't ask you who they were for. I asked you where you got them.'

There was a vase of pink roses on the dining-room table. The waxen blooms reflected in the French polish. Lucy thinking of wake rooms of her childhood, the scent of floors, dark polished wood, undertones of decay.

'From the garden beside Father's office.'

'You're not allowed there.'

'I wanted flowers for Mother.'

'There's nothing in that garden, Doris Curran. The winter has it stripped bare.'

'There were some put away in the shed.'

'Fresh-cut roses in the middle of winter?'

'They hide them from everyone.'

'Who told you that, Doris Curran? Who did you see in the garden?'

'I seen not a soul.'

'You are a wicked child, Doris Curran, the very spawn of darkness.'

'That is God's honest truth.'

'Child, I lived in Female Segregated my first years in this place and there was them in it as could lie before they opened their mouths, and I fear I am not hearing the truth from you.'

'I told you.'

'Be that as it may, if it is found out that I so neglected my duty as to let you stray into that Gethsemane then I will be sent back to Female Segregated without hope of reprieve.'

'I won't tell anyone. As long as Mother gets the flowers.'

'You promise there was no one?'

'I never saw a soul.'

'If I am put back in a cell then you will be sent away to school. There is no one else to care for you.'

Lucy looked at the roses. Doris saw her bless herself quickly. As though there was something profane about the blooms. As if something unholy was abroad in the dark room.

Doris watched Lucy leave. The smell of the roses filled the room, flowers placed beside a fresh-dug grave, wreaths laid on the grave spoil. It was coming night and the klaxon had sounded from Male Medical to return all to their cells. Saucy Jack was watching her. His blue eyes could see through all that was placed in their way. She had not told a lie. She had said to Lucy that she had not seen a soul and had not. For there were those without souls in whom the light of mercy did not shine.

Seventeen

AUGUST 1949

The decision to retry Taylor was announced in the week following his acquittal. The retrial was set for 24th October. The Belfast Newsletter reported that Attorney General Curran was 'anxious' to 'see justice done'.

'Placed the whole thing right at his door,' Ferguson said.

'Where he wanted it placed,' Harvey said.

'He's looking for a fair trial.'

'Please, Mr Ferguson,' Harvey said. 'Your newly acquired interest in justice is commendable. Perhaps you'd like to pull the lever when they drop Taylor through the trap door.'

'Curran will hang him this time.'

'You have to find a way to stop him.'

'Why would he stop? He's Attorney General.'

'A position he will rot in if he persists in this course.'

'There's the stick, Harvey. Where's the carrot?'

Harvey laughed. An arid bark. 'You think Curran would sabotage the case on the promise of preferment?'

'Not Curran. Me.'

'You didn't do very well the first time around, Harry. A hung jury was most unsatisfactory.'

'Bloody McKenzie. That's what comes of sending a boy to do a man's job.'

'So what man are you going to send this time?'

'Myself. I'm sending myself.'

'Very well, Ferguson. There's a seat on the bench in it for Curran if you get a satisfactory outcome.'

'And for me?'

'What do you want?'

'The corporation solicitor would do me fine.'

'You drive a hard bargain. Make sure you're more than just another backstreet blowhard. We've already got too many of those.'

'I won't let you down.'

'I thought letting people down was what the likes of you and I did. Lunn will want the job when it comes up.'

'I can deal with Lunn.'

They were crossing the main hall of the museum. It was the beginning of autumn. Dead leaves blown through the doors were made animate by the wind and the hall of limestone and basalt was filled with a dry scuttling.

'You haven't asked about Takabuti, Ferguson.'

'That damned thing. Gives me the creeps every time I think about it.'

'You should come and see her in her new home. She's really rather gorgeous.'

'I'll give it a miss.'

'Our most popular exhibit.'

'She ended up in the right city, that's for sure.'

There were footsteps on the staircase. Ferguson looked up. Patricia and her friend Hilary were coming down the stairs. Hilary waved to him. 'There's your Mr Ferguson, Patricia.' She came over to them. Patricia followed. She was pale and gave

Ferguson a wan smile, biting her lip.

'We've just been to see the mummy. She gave old Patricia here quite a turn.'

'Some people find her quite disturbing,' Harvey said.

'I can't see it myself. She seemed perfectly deceased and dried up. Reminded me of our French teacher, only more fun.'

'I thought it was hideous,' Patricia said, raising her head. There were two spots of red high on her cheeks.

'Why do you say that, Patricia?' Ferguson said.

'She felt cruel. Evil.'

'My friend has a very active imagination, whereas I see the good in everybody. Calm your overactive imagination, Patricia Curran. It's not like the wall-eyed old biddy is going to follow us home or anything.'

Ferguson watched Patricia. He wanted to tell her that the princess had already followed him home. He knew what she was. She shuffled in. She came unbidden to his dreams, the bejewelled princess, scented with gravemust.

Ferguson and Harvey went with them to the door and watched as the two girls walked off in the autumn evening, the noise of the city stilled for a moment, a premonitory hush. At the iron scaffold of the Palm House Patrica stopped and looked back.

'It's a pity the father isn't more like the daughter,' Harvey said.

'Why do you say that?'

'Because you can scare her and you can't scare him.'

When Esther came home Ferguson was in the dining room with papers and books spread out on the table. Transcripts, law reports, jury lists. Working his way through murder trials in far-off cities, doctrines handed down from medieval courts, the doings of beadles and sheriffs, the law scratched on to parchment. The defences of automatism, of diminished responsibility. Regina versus McNaughton. Regina versus White. Statutes and cases. All this gathering of lore coming down to one thing, a body on the floor, blood pooling.

Esther put her hand on his shoulder. He could smell gin.

'I wonder if I could sentence a man to hang?'

'What are you trying to say?'

'Nothing. Just something Harvey said today.'

'If the price was right you could hang a man, Harry. What are you looking at? Taylor?'

She leaned over him so that he could feel the warmth of her body through her coat.

'I'm trying to find a defence for him but I'm not having any luck.'

She shifted so that he could no longer feel her weight. It was her way of reminding him. Of consents given in the past, the old carnal permissions. Reminding him that they were both entitled to memory.

'What about the jury?'

'I daren't try it twice. Curran realised what happened first time around.'

'Afterwards then.'

'What do you mean?'

'Sometimes you think you're doing the right thing. Everything's under control. And then it all unravels.'

'You might be right. Maybe I'm looking in the wrong place.'

'Glad to be of help.'

'You should go to bed. I might be here for a while.'

Ferguson heard his wife's feet on the floor above him. He imagined the clothes flung on a chair, the rustling undergarments, Esther walking barefoot across the floor, picturing the ankle, the bare instep. He imagined placing his fingers on the back of her neck, the inside of her wrist, chaste touches. He heard the bed creak and then there were no more noises. He worked on until dawn. He went upstairs and opened Esther's door. He went over to the bed and looked down at her. She was making small, troubled noises. He thought of Patricia that day. He wondered what was troubling his wife, a haggard visitant in gravecloth. He smoothed her hair and kissed her forehead. She did not wake.

He went into his own room and opened the curtains. He placed his head against the cool glass. Wind tossed the trees on the street. Light from the shipyard reflected on black storm clouds, a dull industrial flare. Ferguson lay down on the bed and slept. He woke at nine and went downstairs. He telephoned Lunn's office and made an appointment to see the solicitor.

*

Patricia had arranged to play tennis on Saturday morning. When she returned at four o'clock she went to the scullery. She put her racket in its wooden press and tightened the frame around it. She slipped a packet of ten Black Cats from under the washstand and broke the cellophane. She had taken a match and a piece of striker from the house. She struck and cupped the match to light the cigarette. There was a mirror on the door of the cabinet above the mangle and she watched herself in it. She liked the way that Esther Ferguson smoked, the way she struck world-weary poses, narrowed her eyes to look through the smoke. There were ways of holding yourself that Patricia was anxious to learn. Hilary said she looked like a courtesan when she smoked. She said she should be wearing something diaphanous, something sheer and revealing.

She turned at a sound. Desmond was standing in the doorway.

'You should put that out.'

'Says who?'

'Mother's looking for you. She's on the warpath.'

'I haven't done anything.'

'It's the talk of the town, Mother says.'

'What is, for goodness' sake?'

'You and the Douglas girl. Down in the Stranmillis graveyard with the entire Campbell rugby team if you believe half of what you hear.'

'And do you, Desmond?'

'Do I what?'

'Believe what you hear?'

'All I know is you're going to catch it. Particularly since Father's trial is starting on Monday. All he needs is for the jury to hear that the Attorney General's daughter is a creature of the lowest kind.'

'I'm nothing of the sort, Desmond, and you know it.'

'I'm only repeating what Mother said.'

'I'm not surprised since you're incapable of having an opinion of your own.'

Her brother stepped into the scullery and closed the door behind him. He spoke coldly.

'I do have an opinion of my own, Patricia. I have a very firm opinion about you.'

'I thought you might.'

'Mother said she wants to see you in her bedroom at five.'

'I shan't go.'

'That would not be a good idea.'

'It's the only one I can think of.'

'You can't run away from every problem.'

'It's you that runs away, Desmond. To your university and handing out leaflets and your rotten old Moral Rearmament.'

'I used to think that Hilary Douglas was a bad influence on you. Now I think it's the other way round.'

'Send me a leaflet. I'll think about the error of my ways.'

'Please, Patricia. You know what Mother's like. It'll be worse if she smells tobacco from you.'

'That's rich. You gave me my first puff. That summer in Mourne. On the hillside behind the old house.'

'So I did.'

She put her hand on his arm. Lost in the sunlit uplands of childhood. Desmond and Patricia had been left alone with a housekeeper. There had been boating trips. Roaming through fields. Minnows in jars.

'Was there a dog who went everywhere?' Patricia wondering if she had dreamed it. A characterful half-breed with wiry hair and a quizzical tilt to its head.

'There was a dog. Nipper.' Desmond looking at her, suddenly eager for any allurements that were on offer, half-recalled affections. On the night of Patricia's murder he was to find her corpse and raise it from the ground and proclaim that there was life within although the body was cold and stiff. Following the trial and conviction of Iain Hay Gordon for the murder, and the incarceration of his mother in an asylum, Desmond left the bar to become a missionary priest. He worked for five decades in South African townships where he acquired a reputation for courage in confronting apartheid. Growing old in the close-packed shanties. Listening to the night winds on the veldt.

Patricia ground the cigarette out beneath her heel and picked up the butt.

'I'll go to Mother,' she said. She touched his arm as she left the scullery.

Patricia knocked on her mother's door and opened it. Doris was sitting at her dressing table. She did not look round. Her sewing basket was open at her side.

'You wanted me, Mother?'

'I have heard disgraceful reports of your behaviour. That a mother should have to listen to such things about her own daughter.'

'I haven't done anything wrong, Mother.'

'I suppose smoking isn't wrong. I can smell it from here. Where did you get the cigarettes? Down at the graveyard with some unsuitable young man. I hope that's all you got from him.'

'Mother. Don't speak to me like that, please.' Patricia catching the tone-shift in her mother's voice, trying to see her face in the dressing-table mirror. *That's the way to talk. That'll put manners on the little vixen.*

'Them's the boys to do damage to a girl. Them's the saucy boys.'

'Mother, please. You're frightening me.'

'You don't frighten too handy.'

'I promise I won't go near the graveyard again, Mother. I promise.'

'Come over here.' Patricia crossed the room until she stood beside her mother. Doris took hold of her right wrist and bent it back.

'You're hurting me. Please.'

'The world is full of hurt. It's about time you knew it.'

Patricia heard car wheels on the gravel outside.

'Father's home.' But Lance Curran never came home early on a Saturday evening. Doris kept her head turned away. Patricia glimpsed her eyes in the mirror and they seemed devoid of human expression. She twisted in an effort to escape but Doris's grip did not weaken.

Ferguson got out of his car and looked up at the bedroom window above the front door. The curtains were red and the two women were backlit. It was difficult to put meaning to their movements. He went to the door and took hold of the bell pull. Within the house a brass bell made toll. In the room above the door Doris released Patricia. The girl backed away from her, holding her wrist. When Doris turned from the mirror her face was white and there was a drop of blood on her mouth where she had bitten her lip.

'Take me away from here,' she said, 'take me away from this house.'

'Oh Mother,' Patricia said.

Ferguson had intended to visit Lunn at home that evening. He had driven through the Shankill and Sandy Row. Groups of men stood on street corners and watched the car as it passed.

The road to the Malone area took him into the environs of the university and of the museum. He told himself he did not believe in succubi or their pomps but he wished that his route did not take him past the grey museum building and the mummy blind in the tomb dark.

He had ordered police posted at the bottom of the Malone Road earlier that day and had expected to see a tender but he saw none. The message was clear. Curran had sought to go alone on this case and he had been granted his wish.

The mansions of the wealthy stood on the Malone hill, the terracing below them erected on the mudflats and silt beds of the estuarine plain, the ground on which they stood wet and disease-prone, shallow sea to the east, open marshland to the south.

On his way up the hill he saw several groups of young men. Older men stood behind them, backed into the gateways of the large houses, under the shadow of old-growth wisteria and holm oak in the gardens behind them as though they were kernes summoned from the treeline by woodcraft.

Ferguson stopped at a phone box halfway up the Malone Road, but the bakelite receiver had been snapped in half and the copper and zinc wiring loom had been stripped from its tin box and now lay on the ground. He got back into the car and drove to Curran's. On his way he saw Desmond driving down the road in the company of a man he knew to be part of the Moral Rearmament movement.

Ferguson rang the doorbell again. Desmond was gone and Curran's car was not in the driveway but he had seen the two women's figures at the window though they were now gone. He heard laughter from the roadway. He raised his fist to beat on the door before Patricia opened it. There was a scratch on her cheek. Her eyes were dark and unreadable.

'I need your telephone,' he said. She did not move and he pushed past her.

'Who are you calling?' she said.

'Sir Richard Pim. Inspector of Constabulary. Who is in the house?'

'Mother is upstairs. She isn't feeling well.'

Ferguson spoke into the receiver.

'Pim?'

'Harry Ferguson. I thought I might hear from you tonight.' Pim lived in Hillsborough, outside the city. Ferguson pictured the oak-lined hallway. The tree-lined avenue.

'There's mischief afoot on the Malone Road tonight.'

'You interrupted an interesting hand of bridge, Ferguson. I'll presume you don't play.'

'I don't think the boys I saw coming up the road were looking for a game of bridge either.' Ferguson reminding himself to tone it down. Pim was a friend of Winston Churchill.

'Sometimes it's best to let the mob have its head.'

'There's more than Judge Curran living on the Malone Road. Many's the man won't be best pleased that you let these boys out of their box. Just bear in mind, Pim, it's harder to get them back in than let them out.'

'As long as Lancelot Curran understands his position.'

'You've made your point, Mr Pim. I'm standing in the Attorney General's hallway. There's only his wife and sixteen-year-old daughter here.'

Pim sighed. Ferguson had heard rumours that he was in poor health. He had seen him in the Reform Club. A slight man with sandy hair, dandyish, malevolent.

'I'll send the cavalry, Ferguson, but be a good fellow and try to persuade the judge.'

'I have a few ideas as to how to deal with this.'

'I'm sure you do, Harry. I'm sure you do.'

Pim hung up. Ferguson replaced the receiver.

'You're shaking,' Patricia said.

'Am I? People like Pim have that effect on me. Are all the doors locked?'

'Yes. Desmond insists when the ladies are alone in the house. Are we in diffs?'

'Not now. The police are on their way. Still would be a good idea to stay away from the windows for ten minutes. I'm going to move my car around the back.'

Ferguson stepped out into the night. Patricia stood behind him. The wind moved the trees. Leaves gathered in the angle of the porch. Ferguson remembered the leaves on the floor of the museum. The dry scuttling. A man moved from the shadow of the gate pillars. A flung granite sett struck the windscreen of his car and span obliquely from the starring glass, hitting Ferguson above the eye. Dazed, he went to his knees. He felt Patricia beside him.

'Go back inside,' he said.

'Bugger that for a game of soldiers,' she said, trying to lift him. From the south a siren sounded.

'Tell the Attorney,' a man shouted, 'hang Taylor and we'll fucking hang him.'

Another siren sounded from the bottom of the road. They heard running feet. A third siren began and the noise of the approaching tenders sounded together like some iron klaxon announcing a new coming. Patricia helped Ferguson up and into the house. In the hallway she looked at his eye.

'You need something on that. It's split open. Clean though. You need the doctor.'

'No doctor.'

'Let me look after it then.'

'What about your mother?'

'She'll be all right. She had one of her turns. She always sleeps like the dead afterwards.'

Ferguson held his handkerchief to his cut eye. Patricia led him towards the back of the house through the sculleries and outhouses. She left him in a scullery lined with tennis rackets, hockey sticks with worn grips, tennis shoes. He had not thought of her as sporting. He imagined her moving in the scuffed tennis shoes, up on her toes, at full stretch.

She came back with mercurochrome and lint. She washed the cut and swabbed it with the mercurochrome.

'Does it sting?' she said.

'Yes.'

'Death, where is thy sting. Grave, where is thy victory.'

'You make it sound like a song.'

'Bloody Sunday school. I shouldn't say bloody. Especially about Sunday school. My language is appalling. Everyone says so.'

She cut gauze from a roll and pressed it over the cut.

'You look like a boxer. Jack Dempsey or somebody.' She took the Black Cats out from under the sink, lit two and handed one to him.

'I'm not helpless.'

'I like men's company. I like doing things for them. Will

those idiots come back?'

'No. Not with the police here.'

Rain blew against the scullery windows. Patricia shivered.

'That's all the better. Rain keeps them off the streets.'

'It's cold out here.'

'Your cut is bleeding again.' She made him sit and put the cigarette in the corner of her mouth, narrowing her eyes against the smoke as she took a fresh piece of gauze and pressed it against the wound. He was aware of her throat, the inner part of her wrist, the shadow of her underarm where the fabric of her blouse parted. She put her knee against his thigh to steady herself so that her skirt fell away from her knee, her body all underside and vulnerable points. He could feel the weight of her leg against his thigh, the womanly substance of it. She took the gauze from the cut and looked at him. An older man. The rumpled suit. Scented with tobacco and cologne. Worldly. The allure of the corrupted. Knowing what he'd bargained away. The soul's carnage. She held his eyes with her own dark stare. He could not turn away from her look. The mesmeric void.

Across the city watchfires burned on street corners. In the Corn Market street preachers spoke of that which was set aside and could not be taken up again.

Eighteen

Lily stayed with her sister until the appeal was heard. Her mother said that the case was a judgement on her and that the child inside her would ballast her life in regret. She said the walk up the hill to the Crumlin Road prison would be as the hill of Golgotha. She did not know how things had changed for Lily. The city felt strange to her now. She had become someone different in the courtroom. The woman in mourning black. Nodded at, deferred to. She was a carrier of some storied force she barely understood. People stood aside for her. They stopped talking when she went into shops, carried her bags. There was a weight of expectation around her, a grave attention.

In the visiting area she sat across a table from Taylor. He looked strained, hollow-eyed. The seams of his jacket were coming apart where he had unpicked the stitches. He wanted to know if the police had come to his house again, whether they had looked in his box of tricks? He told her that he had asked to see the gallows.

'What did you do that for?'

'I wanted to see how it works. But the warder says it's all just a pile of timber against the wall. They build it up when they need it. The hangman brings the rope and pinnings with him in a black case.' He rubbed his thumb and forefinger together as though he could feel the rope between his fingers, the hemp and sisal twist, the hurting coarseness of it.

'Curran's prosecuting again. I'd put a rope around his neck and hoist him high. I'd see his lordship's legs kicking, so I would.'

'He brings his daughter into the courtroom with him,' Lily said. She knew to go along with him. She knew that if she didn't agree with him he would remember it.

'I seen her sitting and talking with some boy in a suit. Her like a tramp.'

'She thinks she is somebody,' Lily said.

'There's him twisting every word I'm saying and throwing it back at me.'

'You should get Mr Hanna to talk more for you,' Lily said. 'Everybody knows you been done down.'

'They'll know it well enough when I make the acquaintance of Harry Allen.'

'Who's he?'

'The hangman. You'd think you would know that.'

'I don't want to think about things like that, Robert.'

'It would be the best part of you to think it, for if Mr Hanna doesn't pull his socks up I'll be shaking hands with Mr Allen on the way up them wooden stairs.'

Lily wanted to tell him about how things had changed. How she walked abroad now bathed in some shadowy grace. That she had fallen into the city's favour. On Saturdays her sister's husband drove them to Bangor. They'd link arms and walk along the front. People would notice her. The girl Robert Taylor's engaged to. The sisters would sit in the flat-roofed shelters on the front, people passing and looking. They'd heard about the black-veiled girl in court.

Taylor sensed this from her. He felt she'd taken something

that belonged to him. The prison was a place of iron and basalt. Brass locks and plain cut stonework. He could try to work into the substance of it until his fingers bled but it yielded nothing of itself to him. He walked through the prison surly and badgered. When Lily came he wanted to pinch and probe. When the warders weren't looking he kicked her under the table. The kicks were hard and spiteful. Her calves and shins were covered in bruises when she got home. You'd be better off if they hung that creature, her mother said, if he was a dog they'd shoot him.

Lily took out the waist of the black dress to fit her so that she could wear it at the retrial. The baby was due in November. Each night before she went to bed Lily sat in front of the mirror without make-up. Her face was pale and bloodless. She placed the black veil on her head and let it fall. She saw herself standing outside Crumlin Road in the frozen dawn. Her sister said they hoisted a black flag over the prison when the deed was done. She thought of the warden posting Taylor's execution notice on the wooden doors, the gasp of the crowd, the widow of the hanged man standing before the gaol, elevated beyond them, a figure of blood and vengeance, a soothsayer, to raise a trembling finger, bring down curses, old malfeasances.

*

A policeman waved Ferguson through the gates of Lunn's house. There were formal gardens beyond the gate pillars, topiaries, a walled garden, crafted beds. Lunn met him at the bayed front of the house and they took the yew walk, the graveyard tree, dense and heavy, small poisonous berries in branch crooks.

'I thought Curran would have thrown in the towel. I thought he'd shown what he is made of. Made a fool out of Hanna. Made a fool out of all of us. I thought that would have done him.'

'Curran's never done.'

'If he keeps on he'll bring the whole house of cards down around all of us.'

'That wouldn't be a bad thing.'

'I take it you don't want to go back to riveting ship hulls at the yard, Ferguson, because that's where this will take you.'

'I have his measure.'

'You've a reputation as a man that can deliver. I haven't seen evidence.'

'I will end this.'

'How?'

'My business. There's a trade.'

'What?'

'A seat on the bench for Curran.'

'Not in my gift.'

'I know that.'

'What else?'

'The solicitor's post.'

'For you.'

'Yes.'

'Have you spoken to your wife of your ambition?'

'Why?

'The dinners you have to attend, Ferguson. The agricultural shows. The gala balls. I hear tell Mrs Ferguson is took bad with the nerves.'

'That's my concern.' But Ferguson could see himself in the future. A hunched figure in a raincoat. A carrier of secrets. People's secret lives. Their inner corruptions. If there was a realm of bad faith he would be its king and potentate.

'It's a deal, Ferguson, if that's really what you want.'

'Tell Pim to keep a watch on the Curran house.'

'I heard there was something the other night all right.'

'The two women were in the house on their own.'

'The Currans are never on their own when you're around.' Ferguson wondering what Lunn was driving at.

'By the way, I hear Lance Curran was seen in a betting shop in Warrenpoint yesterday. You need to keep a closer eye on your man, not just his wife and daughter. If he has to go to a betting shop then he's out of credit with his bookmaker. Between ourselves, it's no commendation for a man who desires to sit on a judge's bench.'

Ferguson stopped at a telephone box and rang the Curran house. Desmond answered. Ferguson hoping it would be Patricia.

'Is your father there?'

'He didn't come home last night, Mr Ferguson. Mother is in a frightful state. He's due in court tomorrow, isn't he?'

Ferguson hung up. He rang the Reform Club. They hadn't seen Curran for several days. He rang shopfront bookmakers in towns within a twenty-mile radius. He bought a Telegraph, checked the races and rang around the courses, dog and horse. Ferguson knew the track touts and bookies' runners. They'd pick a man like Curran out of the race crowd. They'd pick him out of any crowd. Curran had been seen in Downpatrick late on Saturday afternoon.

'He was laying down the cash,' the source said, 'playing like a twelve o'clock man in a nine o'clock town.'

Ferguson hung up. He dialled a number in Whiteabbey. Curran's bookmaker, Hughes.

'My name's Harry Ferguson. I am a business acquaintance of Lancelot Curran's.'

'I know who you are, Mr Ferguson.'

'I need to know Mr Curran's position with you.'

'Mr Curran's position is different to the way it was six months ago.'

'Why's that?'

'He was the coming man then.'

'He's still the coming man.'

'Not since the Taylor case. Curran's starting to look like a beaten docket.'

'Taylor won't hang.'

'If you say so, Mr Ferguson. In the meantime Mr Curran's at full stretch. Don't get me wrong. If I was in the dock I'd want Curran on my side, and I hope he hangs Taylor and I'll join him in dancing on the grave. But in the meantime he's gone as far as he can with me.'

That night the telephone rang in the hallway. Ferguson got out of bed. It was after midnight, the hallway parquet cold on his bare feet. It was Patricia.

'Father's home.'

'Did he tell you where he was?'

'No.'

'I'm frightened, Harry.'

'There's no need.'

Patricia didn't answer. The phone went dead. Ferguson with the receiver to his ear. Seeing Patricia replacing the device into its cradle, the smooth, handled instrument. Ferguson left alone with the line hum, the night depths sounded.

Nineteen

MARCH 1961

Sometimes Doris liked to see Ferguson come and sometimes she found it tiresome. He was a big padding man who looked as if he put on regret every morning like a suit of clothes. They made you feel sorry for them and then they tricked you.

Lance was not like that. She did not think that Lance regretted anything in his life.

Ferguson asked her if he could piece together the night that Patricia was lost. Lost was the word he used. As though Patricia had wandered off. As though she had gone out into the woods and had strayed off the path into the shadow of the trees.

Ferguson pestered. Lucy knew what to do with a pestering man and no mistake. There's plenty in the wards were all hands. For all they were insane they knew where to grab a girl if they were let.

'Mrs Curran,' Ferguson went on, 'what happened on the day Patricia died? Did you go anywhere, for instance?'

'I played bridge with several neighbours. Mrs Whyte, Mrs Denvir and the doctor's wife, Mrs Wilson, between the hours of two o'clock and four o'clock.'

'You remember it very well.'

'We played in Mrs Denvir's drawing room. The day was dark. It began to rain as her mantel clock struck three. She served tea. The tea set was Spode.'

Card games in provincial drawing rooms, night drawing in. Four figures stilled around the green baize card table, the sound of a coal shifting in the fire, rain against the windowpane. Events sinking into their own myth and history.

'What time did you leave?'

'I left at four o'clock. Mrs Wylie offered to drive but I said I would walk. It wasn't far. A mile.'

Doris had tied a scarf tightly around her head. It was a wild evening. Not yet dark. The trees strained and wet twigs broke underfoot on the pavement. Seabirds blown in from the salt marshes and wintering grounds. White shapes picked out in the stormlight against the black trees.

Doris taking twenty minutes to walk the mile from the Denvir house to the gate lodge of the Glen.

'Did you meet anyone on the way?'

'I was alone.' A solitary figure walking on the land side of the road because it was less exposed to the weather than the sea wall side. Passing the empty phone box, its lit windows sentinel against the growing dusk. Turning into the driveway of the Glen, into the avenue of trees, the woods as Patricia called them.

'Did you see anyone on your way up the avenue? Someone in the trees or anything like that?'

After Patricia was murdered, paperboy George Chambers gave evidence that he thought he had seen someone in the undergrowth, that he felt there was someone watching him and that he had heard footsteps in the dead leaves under the trees. Chambers said that he had walked up the driveway at 5.45 p.m., an hour and twenty-five minutes after Doris Curran said she had arrived at the Glen, and twenty-five minutes after Patricia got off the Belfast bus on the main road. Chambers's statement had never been corroborated. When Capstick had forced a confession from Iain Hay Gordon his statement had been dismissed. It was said that Chambers enjoyed the attention in court and had allowed his imagination to run away with him. But Ferguson remembered Chambers in the interrogation room at Whiteabbey police barracks where he had given his initial statement. The boy intent, trying to pick out detail. At what point in the driveway did he become aware of a presence in the trees? Were the footsteps ominous, a shuffling killer's gait? Did he hear anything other than footsteps? Was there harsh breathing?

'I saw Mrs McCrink.' The housekeeper leaving the house, trying to get home before dark. The housekeeper had said she had spoken to Doris but that she had not replied.

'You got to the house.'

'I had lost my key and my husband had not given me another. I climbed in through the downstairs bedroom window.'

The back bedroom cold and disused. A smell of damp bedclothes in it. If the chronology of the night's events was correct Patricia was walking towards Oxford Street bus station in Belfast with John Steel.

'I went to the cloakroom. I took my wet coat off and put it on a hanger.'

'Was there a car at the house?'

'My car was there.'

'The Ford Popular?'

'Yes.'

'Were there any telephone calls around that time?'

Doris waited for Lucy to say something. Keep your cakehole

shut, lass, can you not see what he's about? Don't trust him, he's the devil. But Lucy did not speak. Jack did not speak. Jack watched.

'Mrs Curran, I think Patricia might have called for a lift. She didn't like walking up the drive on her own. It was her habit to telephone from the box at the end of the avenue for someone to go down for her in the car.'

'Patricia was a wilful girl. She did as she wanted.'

'But she was scared. She had been attacked on the driveway before. A strange man.'

'How did you know that?' Doris turned to look at Ferguson. Good girl, Lucy said, give him what for.

'What?'

'How did you know that someone scared Patricia?'

'I don't know. Perhaps your husband mentioned it.'

'Judge Curran did not discuss what happened.' *So how does he know?* Jack says. *How does Harry Ferguson know that hands reached for Patricia in the dark?*

Ferguson had been woken by the phone. The black telephone standing on a table placed on the parquet. Cold to the touch. There was a dire sound to its ringing. You thought of beacons lit, watchmen straining to hear, the night alarm sounding.

The phone stopped before he got out of bed. He heard Esther's voice. When he went down to the hallway she handed the receiver to him.

'It's for you.' She had been sitting on her own in the dark, drinking. One shoe was off. There was a bottle of brandy on the card table, a filled ashtray, a glass on its side. Wayposts of the fallen.

'Hello?'

'Harry, it's Patricia, can you help me?' She sounded exhausted. He'd heard the tone in men's voices after fighting. That sleepy note. They ceded to things. They lay down in the mud and died.

'Where are you?'

'In Whiteabbey. At the park.'

'I'll be there in thirty minutes.'

He went upstairs and dressed. When he came downstairs he could see Esther's face lit by the glow of a cigarette.

'Where are you going?'

'Whiteabbey.'

'Why?'

'You heard. Lance Curran's daughter. She's got herself into a scrape.'

'Watch out for her, Ferguson. She's a trollop. Takes one to know one.'

'Try to go to sleep, Esther.'

'Maybe the mother's the same. The apple never falls far from the tree.'

Ferguson found Patricia sitting in the corner of the bandstand. It was frosty, the park grass crisp under his feet. He took off his suit jacket and put it around her.

'What happened?'

'I sneaked out of the window. Hilary's father was away and she took his car. A bit of a lark. We just drove around, then she stopped at the end of the drive and walked up with me. I was going to climb back in the back bedroom window.'

'What time?'

'It must have been half one. We went up the drive. There wasn't a sound. There was freezing fog in the woods. I thought I heard something.'

Night vapours in the trees. A fox barks in the parkland. A twig breaks.

'Did you see anything?'

'No. I heard a man breathing. Feet in the trees. We started to run. Hilary said there were two of them but I only saw one.'

A fleeing girl. A man bursting from the trees. He's been crouched there in the feral dark. Her hair streams out behind her as she runs. She turns to double back towards the road. He catches her and grasps her arm. Without turning around she swings her arm. She plays tennis and squash. He grunts in pain and lets go. Patricia running on the avenue with a sprinter's grace, arms pumping, muscular and fleet.

'You didn't see his face?'

'No. And he didn't say anything. I made Hilary stop the car to call you. She dropped me here.'

'You're shivering.'

'Put your arms around me.' He sat down beside her and put his arm over her shoulders. She put her head against his chest. She fell asleep. Trusting to the world the way adolescents did. The way they made the world fit them. The way they sprawled, propped themselves in old summer bandstands and bus shelters, rawboned, looselimbed. They lost themselves in the textures of things, grateful for the fabric of the world. Ferguson let her sleep, his legs folded awkwardly under him. He thought that they did not fear death. They did not run away when they saw it coming. They thought that it could be bargained with. That you could parlay with the shadows.

He let her sleep for twenty minutes, then woke her. They drove along the front. Ferguson stopped at a phone box and called the house. Curran answered. Ferguson told him what had happened. He suggested that Curran call the police at Whiteabbey and have them search the woods. They drove up the avenue and stopped outside the house.

'You'd better go in now.' He felt Patricia put her hand on his shoulder. She rested her face against his neck for a moment. That downturned mouth. She opened the door and got out and walked towards the steps at the front of the house. He felt the imprint of her lips against his neck, warm scapular of regret on his skin.

The door opened as she reached it. Lance Curran framed in the hall door, backlit, a staged presence. Levers creaking, ropefall through pulleys. Painted backdrops falling into place.

Ferguson wound down his window.

'Do you want me to call at the police station on the way home?'

'No. I'll call,' Curran said. Patricia slipped past him in the doorway. Curran turned after her and closed the door.

After he had left her at the house Ferguson stopped the car and looked for traces of the lurking man in the beam of the headlights but the ground was frozen solid. There were no footprints in the driveway gravel or on the muddy grass at the margin between the driveway and the woods. Ferguson thought that he was being watched. He looked up at the house.

In late November 1952, following Patricia's murder, Ferguson inspected that night's log at Whiteabbey RUC station. The incident had not been reported.

'Perhaps it was you,' Doris said.

'I'm sorry?'

'The man who attacked her. Perhaps it was you.'

'Really, Mrs Curran, I wouldn't ever have done anything to hurt Patricia.'

Ask him why not? Jack spoke. Lucy shrank back.

Ask him why not?

'Why would you not hurt her, Mr Ferguson?'

'Because she was a pleasant young person of my acquaintance, Mrs Curran.'

'By Jesus you were acquainted with her all right.'

'Please, Mrs Curran.'

'Who was it that drove her home the night she said she was attacked on the avenue? The man that chased her on the driveway wasn't the only one laid hands on her that night, I'll lay a bet on that.'

'I'm not sure if this is getting us anywhere.'

'Who was driving the car?'

'What car?'

'The damn car that brought her home.'

'I was.'

'Did she show her true nature?'

'I'm not sure what you mean.'

'Did the girl make free with her person?'

'I think that's enough for today.'

'Did she charver you in the front seat of the car?'

Charver. Ferguson had heard the word used by the East End conscripts in his battalion. Charvering the West End tarts on a Saturday night.

'The poxy bitches have the streets ruined.' Doris was sitting back in the chair, her knees apart, in a mannish sprawl. 'You'd get half an hour in the saddle for the price of a split loaf.'

'You think Patricia was like that?'

Ferguson had been sent alone into cells to interview imprisoned Nazis. The lieutenants and gauleiters, brooding henchmen. The interrogation cells were cold, snow on the ground outside. They barely seemed to know he was there. They seemed to be staring past him to scenes of atrocity in their past. He knew that if they chose to attack him the Russian guards would not unlock the cell door in time. They were death's familiars. Jeopardies he did not know the names of hung in the air. You had to press on with your task. You fumbled with the papers, asked the questions out of sequence. Were you present when? Did you command a named squad? Were you gauleiter in charge of this place or that, of the emptied districts, the ghettoes and the bone cities? If they did not answer you noted the refusal. Not answered, they said. *Not answered.*

The person sitting opposite him knew this. The person sitting opposite him smiled. Ferguson had seen that kind of smile in Nuremberg. There was a range of grim amusements that were known only to the damned.

'Did Patricia come back to the house on the night of the twelfth of November 1952, Mrs Curran, the night she was murdered?'

Not answered.

'Why did Judge Curran not allow the police into the house

and why did he not allow them to interview the family?'

Not answered.

'Was there a large dried bloodstain on the floorboards in Patricia's room?'

Not answered.

'Why was Patricia's room redecorated in the week following her murder and her belongings burned?'

Not answered.

'Did Judge Curran call John Steel and ask him if he had seen Patricia when in fact the Judge knew that she was dead?'

Not answered.

Doris's posture had changed. Ferguson realised that she was asleep. He unfolded the blanket that lay on her knees and draped it over her, tucking it around her shoulders. He went outside. He wondered if there was a reason why hospitals for the mad were located in such places. Sprawling sites surrounded by marshes and undrained fen. Isolated settlements prone to introspection. He could see the temporary buildings on the perimeter of the site, the Orlits and Nissen huts, looking like abandoned settlements.

He remembered the interviews in Nuremberg. There was a point where the prisoner would start to talk. He never knew the trigger. They gave dates and locations. They gave grid numbers and map references. It was important that no mistakes were made. The depth of their atrocity demanded no less. The dead must be made to answer for their crimes.

Twenty

OCTOBER 1949

On the weekend of 20th October autumn lows crossed the Atlantic, serried ranks of storms. In the harbour mouth sandbars shifted westward and tidal surges grounded ships in the channel mud. Trees were blown down in the city and shops closed early on Saturday as slates and other debris were dislodged from rooftops. By six in the evening the streets were deserted, that season's havocs unleashed.

Harry Ferguson left Leopold Street RUC barracks at nine o'clock. Rain beat against the windscreen and blown leaves whirled in the night wind, crossed in the headlight beam and were torn away into the darkness.

Ferguson met Lunn in the foyer of the Reform Club. Lunn was wearing evening dress. There was a poppy on his lapel.

'Bar Association dinner tonight,' Lunn said.

'I wasn't invited.'

'I hope your news is better than mine. Andrews is going to preside over the retrial.'

'The Lord Chief Justice himself. Taylor should be flattered.'

'Andrews doesn't like me and he doesn't like the way this case has dragged on. He wants it put to bed and Taylor in a hole in the ground. He doesn't see the consequences for everything we've built in this city if Taylor hangs.'

'It's no odds anyway. I spoke to my men tonight.'

'Glenravel Street barracks?'

'No. Don't forget they've spent time with Taylor. They'd be as happy to get him a date with Harry Allen as I would. I went to Leopold Street. They'll do what they're bid and keep their mouths shut.'

'I have to tell Taylor.'

'I don't want you to.'

'I have to. He's ready to fold. Maybe even confess. He saw that black cap sitting on the judge's bench. He isn't fit to face another session in the box with Curran the way things stand.'

'He'll start acting smart. He could bring the whole thing down around all our heads.'

'He won't, as long as your men do what they're told.'

'They will, but I don't want them put in the box. I can't answer for them there.'

'I'll take care of it.'

'If Taylor knows he'll tell it all round the Crumlin Road.'

'He's smarter than that.'

'Could you hide it, Lunn? If you were on trial for your life and a way out appeared?'

'I take your point.'

Cars were arriving at the front of the Reform Club. The Bar Association dinner was being held at the Culloden Hotel and the cars were to take the diners there. Ferguson stood back in the entrance to the porter's lodge as the judges and barristers came down the steps in procession, sequenced according to rank. Ferguson saw Curran walking alone.

'Mrs Curran isn't with him. She must be took bad with the nerves again,' Lunn said. 'If I was married to a man like him I'd be bad with the nerves as well, not to mention the daughter if half the things I hear are true.'

'For a man thought of as hunger's mother in this town, you've plenty to say about other people's families.'

'You'd be better keeping a civil tongue in your head, Ferguson.'

'I have to work with you but I don't have to like you, Lunn.'

Lunn smiled. He joined the ranks of men who waited in order of seniority. Judges appellate and magistrate, Queen's Counsel and ordinary and the subordinate. Men of laws in procession. Ferguson watched them silently as they departed into the night.

*

Taylor had to sit through more hours of coaching with Hanna. He would slip into his cell unannounced, he told Lily. You'd be lying on your bed daydreaming and look up to see Hanna standing there, the screw closing the door behind him. It scared him. Hanna didn't look like the jovial man about town that everyone talked about. One night Taylor woke up to see Hanna standing over him.

'It's late, Mr Hanna,' Taylor said. Hanna put his hands on the bed and leant over Taylor. Taylor could feel spittle in his face when Hanna spoke. 'Get up and put on your clothes, son. If it was up to me I'd let you swing and good riddance, but I've pinned my colours to your sick little mast and you'll be ready for Curran when you step into that courtroom.'

'I told Hanna I didn't need no going through the story. You

know the way I am.'

Lily did know the way he was. He was quick-witted and fast with his tongue. He could say something hurtful and be halfway down the street before what he had said sank in. Sometimes when she said something wrong he would pinch her in passing so quick that no one else saw it, but it left a bruise that took weeks to fade.

'What do we do, Mr Hanna?'

'There's two main things Curran will be going after again. One's the blood on your clothes. The second is the identification evidence. You'll have to deal with the blood. I'll take care of the identification.'

'It looks bad, Mr Hanna. We can't say blood isn't blood and we can't prove the woman didn't see me.'

'We don't have to prove or disprove anything. We just have to make it look as if we did.'

'What do you mean, Mr Hanna?'

'I've never met you, son, and after this I'll never see you again, but I know you better than you know yourself. I know what happened the night you impregnated Lily Jones. You took a gamble that she wouldn't get pregnant but she did. You took a gamble with Mary McGowan and you lost. So what do you do when you lose? Deal the cards again. That's your life, son. You lose, you go on to the next bet. Can't understand the hue and cry. But this time I'm handing you the cards and I'm playing them. Now. Why was there blood on your clothes when you returned to the house?'

'It wasn't blood. It was paint from work.'

'You'll have to do better than that. The police analysed the stains.'

'Nosebleeds. I get these nosebleeds. All the time.'

'That's better. That's the kind of thing I want to hear. Blood on the clothing. Nosebleeds set off by paint fumes?'

'That's it, Mr Hanna.'

The retrial of Robert Taylor for the murder of Mary McGowan opened at Crumlin Road courthouse on 24th October. Lord Chief Justice Andrews presided. Lancelot Curran prosecuted. Robert Hanna QC represented the defence. The storms had not abated. The courthouse yards were littered with storm debris. Seabirds driven inland wheeled in the air above the city. The Lancia was buffeted by the wind as Ferguson drove Curran along the Crumlin Road. As he turned into the courthouse Ferguson saw Lily standing at the top of the steps with Lunn and Hanna to either side of her. Her baby must be due soon. The child's father on trial for his life. The crowd drew back from her, black-clad, charged with sombre force.

When he saw Taylor in the box Ferguson knew that Lunn had told him. Taylor chatted to the warder who brought him in. He waved to members of his family. When the jury were being sworn in he adopted a benign expression. He smiled in an understanding way. He was there to ease them through things. The days ahead would be difficult for all of them but he would stand by them, the twelve members of the jury looking awkward in their best suits and workaday expressions. Lunn wouldn't meet Ferguson's eyes.

Ferguson had seen Patricia once since she went back to school, walking past the university alone, books in her arms, her eyes downcast, looking hunched and scholarly. She had not seen him drive past. He had left a space for her beside him in the public gallery but she did not come.

Lunn did not dispute the evidence of Thornton and the other constables. He wanted to show that he was on their side. That the defence respected the law. When Kathleen McGowan went into the box Curran once more did not spare her. He made her identify the implements of death, the photographs of her mother's injuries, the dress that she had worn in its rich brocade of blood. The witness hesitated at points, averted her gaze from Taylor in the dock and the baleful presence of Lily in the public gallery. It was late afternoon before she had finished, the light falling in wintry tones.

Taylor was to go into the box on the morning of the 24th. The Newsletter said that he 'presented a confident demeanour'. Ferguson thought he looked like some archetype from an old tale. A character you would follow to the edge of the forest, a cheery figure beckoning from under the trees, inviting you to follow him, to go deeper.

Curran settled his papers on the bench and stood without speaking, gathering the attention of the court to him. An usher opened the courtroom door to admit a clerk. A draught blew dead leaves from the foyer into the courtroom and the dead leaves gathered at the base of the the judge's podium.

Curran cross-examined two defence witnesses before Taylor went into the box, prison attendant Robert McAuley and Girvan the prison doctor. They told of two episodes in prison when blood had been found on Taylor's pillow. Taylor had claimed they were nosebleeds caused by the smell of fresh tar from the prison corridors. The doctor said that he found no trace of bleeding from Taylor's ears, nose or throat.

Curran made the two witnesses repeat their testimony.

Taylor's attempt to create a history of nose-bleeding caused by exposure to paint and other substances sounded more transparent on the second telling. Taylor's 'confident demeanour' did not change but his eyes followed Curran everywhere and Ferguson thought he saw something else there, a watcher in the shadows. *Babyface killer.*

Taylor followed McAuley and Girvan into the box. As the two witnesses left the courtroom the draught from the opened door stirred the dead leaves at the foot of the dais and some of the public gallery leaned forward to look, as though they thought some light-footed thing sported on the courtroom parquet.

'Mr Taylor. How long did it take you in your profession as a painter to discover that gloss paint caused your nose to bleed?'

'About two months.'

'Your nose might bleed two or three times a week because of the smell of gloss paint?'

'Well, yes.'

'Did it occur to you that this was not a suitable occupation?'

'No.'

Curran inexorable. None of the rest of Taylor's story held up. Blood was all he had.

'Did you ever suggest to anyone before that it was the smell of gloss paint that caused your nose to bleed?'

'Oh yes.'

'Did you ever suggest it in court?'

'I suggest it today.'

'But until today did you ever suggest it?'

'No.'

'Why did you not think of that before?'

'I wasn't asked.'

'I see.'

'When your attention was drawn to the bloodstains on your coat and the police asked you to account for them you said it was paint?'

'Yes.'

'Why did you tell a lie?'

'I never thought of my nose bleeding.'

'Why didn't you tell them about your nose?'

'I was thinking more of getting out of the barracks.'

'Were you afraid that if you admitted it was blood it would be evidence against you?'

'But I thought it wasn't blood.'

'Wasn't the statement about it being paint a deliberate lie?'

'Yes.'

'You knew it was not paint?'

'Well, it was a brownish colour.'

'Were you asked by the police how the paint got on your foot?'

'Yes, but I never answered them.'

'Why?'

'I was fed up that night.'

'You didn't suggest that the blood came from your nose?'

'No.'

'Why not?'

'I told you. I was fed up that night.' A snarl. Taylor looking as if he wanted to reach out for someone, to get hold of a fleshy part and twist. Ferguson seeing him for what he was. The courtroom seeing him for what he was. The strangler. The pincher and the groper. The keeper of the box of tricks. Curran looked at the judge and raised his eyebrows slightly. Ferguson knew what he was doing. Asking the judge for a recess. You go out on the scene you want your audience to remember. Let it hang in the air. Let it sink in. Judge Andrews considered Taylor. Andrews wanted the conviction. Taylor looked back at him. Placid now.

'Please continue, Mr Curran.'

'The button man.' Patricia slid into the seat beside Ferguson. 'Button eyes and button nose. He's the button man. What did I miss?'

'Your father winning his case.'

'How'd he do that?'

'He took Taylor to the edge of the cliff, then let him throw himself over.'

'Clever Daddy.'

'Very clever.'

'You don't look pleased.'

'There's nothing to be pleased about in this whole thing, Patricia.'

Curran asked the court usher to produce Taylor's overcoat and to show it to the jury. It was the coat Taylor had worn on the morning Mrs McGowan had been killed, when a figure wearing a 'blue coat and yellow shoes' had been seen on Ponsonby Avenue.

'You said the blood got on the coat because you were sleeping in the kitchen with the coat over you.'

'I'd been working at home. I painted two rooms, then I lay down because I was tired.'

'Was the fire lit in the kitchen?'

'Yes.'

'Was it cosy?'

'Yes.'

'If you were cosy as you say you were, what was the necessity to have your overcoat over you?'

'To keep out the draught.'

'Was there a smell of paint in the house?'

'Yes.'

'Where was it coming from?'

'From the front room.'

'You didn't think of closing the kitchen door, although there was a draught?'

'I was just lying down. I wasn't worrying about my nose.'

'Did you not think your nose would bleed?'

'No.'

'Although there was a smell of paint?'

Taylor did not answer. He could not remember what side he had lain on so that the blood got on his overcoat.

'The reason for your difficulty in giving details of this incident is that it never happened at all.'

Taylor was questioned about his claim to have visited the Daisy newsagent at the time of the murder. As with his evidence with regard to painting the house and his nosebleeds in prison, he added detail to his previous testimony, creating new pitfalls for himself. He said he had a conversation with Clarke the newsagent, despite Clarke's denial and Hanna's suggestion that Clarke had left his counter to go to the bathroom. He maintained that he had arranged with Clarke to see him later but then said that he had arranged to meet Billie Booth in the Deer's Head at the same time.

'What's he doing?' Patricia said.

'What do you mean?'

'In the first trial he sounded coached. Like every word that came out of his mouth had been given to him by Lunn. He doesn't sound like that now. It sounds like they've given him his head.'

'You're right,' Ferguson said. Taylor sticking to the script first time round, striking out on his own this time. He couldn't resist it, adding to the narrative, creating new events, stories loaded with harm.

Lily knew what he was doing. He had to find out how it worked, picking at the fabric of his own lies, the densely structured untruths devised in the dark of his cell by Lunn and Hanna. He was cleverer than them. He wanted to take their stories apart and replace them with something ornate, crafted from his box of tricks. She could see how angry Curran was making him and she found herself wondering how he would be if he was acquitted and if he would hurt her or her baby. She placed her hand on her swollen belly and saw the Curran girl watching her, the snobby bitch.

When the jury returned after lunch the foreman asked that they be permittted a break during legal argument. Lunn suggested that they go to Bangor as the previous jury had done. The judge assented and ordered that the jurors be accompanied by officers from Leopold Street barracks.

'You fancy it?' Ferguson said.

'What?'

'The trip to Bangor for the afternoon. Though it's not exactly the weather for it.'

'I like this kind of weather. I'll get the train out. I'll meet you there.'

Ferguson drove out to Bangor. He parked outside the railway station and walked out to the promenade, the wind from the north-east, shingle from the beach driven across the storm walls and on to the concrete. Weed and debris scattered underfoot. Solitary walkers on the sea wall, the sea buoys straining on their cables against the undertows, the tidal flux.

He saw Patricia standing on the sea wall. She was wearing a macintosh, her hands in the pockets. The sea spray had flattened her hair to her forehead. He called up to her, making himself heard above the wind, autumnal, buffeting, not to be denied.

'Come down, Patricia.'

'I like storms.'

'It's not safe. You could be washed off.'

'I feel noble up here. Thinking heroine thoughts.' The swell gathered against the far end of the sea wall and drove along it almost to her feet. The sea spray rose above the wall and fell in grey around her, almost obscured from view, stood on the sea wall, the raincoat to her feet, like a grey-veiled woman from some ghostly telling. Ferguson got on to the wall and took her by the wrist. He pulled her down the stone steps and into the lee of the wall.

'Don't be so rough, Harry,' she said.

'Then don't be foolish.'

'I am a bit damp,' she said.

'You're soaked through,' Ferguson said. 'What train did you come out on?'

'The two thirty.'

'Was the jury on the train?'

'They were. Kind of a mixture. Some of them were having

drinks. The rest looked like church elders. Very sombre and disapproving.'

'Let's go.'

'I need to change. I've got my badminton gear in my bag.'

'You can change in one of the shelters.'

Ferguson led her to one of the concrete-roofed shelters, the damp and chilled interior circled by a wooden bench, names carved in the timber of the seating, hearts pierced with arrows, crude sexual figurings etched into the varnish, the bench an almanac of illicit couplings, the night's doings, the heart abandoned on the margins.

'Turn your back, Harry,' Patricia said. Ferguson could hear her wet clothing fall on the concrete floor, a briskness to her movements, a locker room's utilitarian gestures. Then her bare feet on the floor behind him, her hands over his eyes, the chilled flesh of her forearms against his face.

'Guess who?' She turned him towards her. He kept his eyes on hers, the shadowed gaze, her cold palms on his face, her fingers tracing his jawline, a grave attention brought to bear as though his face were something lain undisturbed for years, a half-sunk artefact dredged from the depths.

'You're starting to get wrinkles, Harry. Here and here. Maybe they're life lines. Do faces have life lines? Does mine?'

'Get dressed, Patricia.' He turned away from her and went to the shelter entrance. He looked down. He could see where her skin had touched the material of his suit, the damp outlined body, the saltwater traces.

They walked up Quay Street into the town. Patricia wore her wet raincoat over her badminton clothes. The wind funnelled through the buildings. There were no day trippers on the streets, one or two locals walking with their heads down.

'What are we looking for?' Patricia said.

'The jury.'

'Where do we look?'

'You said it. Some of them will be in a bar. The rest of them are good-living. They wouldn't go into a public house if their lives depended on it and the weather's not good enough for them to walk.'

'Don't worry, Harry. We'll sleuth them out.'

The amusements and funfair lights were on in the storm dark. The streets were windswept, eerie. They found the jury members clustered like survivors. One group in Shell's tearoom on the front, the rest in the British Legion on Queen's Parade. Ferguson counted how many jurors were in each group. He wrote the figure, the address and time in a notebook.

'What are you up to, Harry?' Patricia said.

'Just making sure that justice is served,' Ferguson said. He walked with her to the train station.

'Do I look tired?' she said.

'No.' But her eyes looked deep-sunk, her cheeks hollow, her hair still damp and flattened to her skull.

'I feel tired. You know Mother is not well?'

'I know that your mother is sometimes quite nervous.'

'Cat on a hot tin roof nervous. I think this trial is making her worse. Sometimes she looks at me like I'm the devil or something. She never does that with Desmond.'

'The trial will soon be over.'

'When I was small I heated the poker in the fire and touched Desmond's leg with it.'

'Did you? Why?'

'I wanted to see what would happen. Desmond forgave me. He's good like that. But I think Mother never forgave me.'

'I'm sure she has.'

'I'd prefer if you didn't answer me at all than answer me like that. She called me Lucy the other night. Do you know who Lucy is?'

'I'm afraid I don't.'

'Mother was brought up in Broadmoor. I wonder if that kind of thing can be catching?'

The train whistle sounded from the platform. She put her lips to his cheek and ran without looking back, disappearing into the crowd.

Ferguson hadn't answered her question about Doris. *If that kind of thing can be catching.*

*

The trial resumed the following morning. In his final cross-examination of Taylor Curran forced him to admit that he had lost all his money at the dog track several days before the murder. Then Curran sought to prove that Taylor had gone to Morrison, the publican, to borrow money before Mary McGowan's death rather than afterwards as Taylor claimed, trying to break the link between Morrison's refusal to lend him money and the subsequent robbery and murder.

Curran was relentless. Taylor's sister Madeleine said that she had accompanied him to see Morrison. Curran destroyed her credibility by proving that she had lied regarding the hiring of the wedding car. Morrison also lied. He said he had met Taylor that afternoon. He said that a girl was waiting for him. Curran asked him to identify the girl. He pointed to Madeleine.

'What was she wearing?'

'I don't know. I took no notice of her.'

'Then how can you be so sure that it was the defendant's sister, six months on?'

Ferguson could feel the silence among the jurors and the public. Witnesses leaving the box, tearstained, harried. They barely listened to Hanna's defence, his description of Taylor as 'almost a boy', his assertion that no normal person would kill for such a pittance. They had eyes only for Curran. Ferguson wondered if he had ever really known Curran or if he could be known. His final witnesses had let their lies be exposed. A long reckoning falling due. When Judge Andrews laid out ten points for the jury to decide, each point was deduced from Curran's reasoning.

Andrews referred to Taylor's attempt to deceive the police by saying that Booth owed him £5. His false statement that he had been to the Daisy. The evidence of the blood. The evidence of Mrs Shiels. The overcoat in the warm kitchen. The blood again, the spilling of it, the damning flow and spatter. The five scratches on Taylor's face, his statement that 'it could have been done by the child'.

Finally the most important question of all. Did Mrs McGowan, that poor lady, tell the truth when she declared on four different occasions, 'Robert did it,' and gave, moreover, the details of how he did it, which precisely corresponded, as I suggest to you, with the nature of the injuries which she received? Was she mistaken?

Counsel said it was a question of mistaken identity. The assailant grasped her by the throat. She had no opportunity of seeing who it was. But according to her, she opened the door and the accused entered and spoke to her and asked for the liberty of using her telephone. It was only then that, according to her, the attack was made upon her. I suggest to you that at that early stage at any rate, she was not distraught and had the opportunity of seeing full well who he was who entered her house. And you will not forget too that, according to her story, if it is true, she had seen him outside only ten minutes before.

The voice that spoke to us in those dying declarations was the voice of Mary McGowan, sitting as she then was, on the edge of eternity. And today, gentlemen, it is for you to say, is not her voice still crying to us from the grave, for justice?

No McKenzie on this jury would stand against the others. The jurors stood up as the judge left the courtroom, white-faced, reserved, as though they had attended a bloody assize from the past. The jurors left for their deliberations. Hanna stood still as his desk. He did not turn to face his adversary. Curran had won.

Twenty-one

In the court precincts leaves blew on the limestone paviours and on the granite kerbing. Patricia had set her back to a stone buttress out of the wind. She was smoking a cigarette. Her father came out of the courtroom with Ellis Harvey. Harvey listened to Curran, then turned and walked slowly away. Curran stood for a moment. The wind tugged at the fabric of his coat. A seagull driven inland rode the courtyard updraft and Curran's eyes followed it upwards as though it rose at his command in its tilt and yaw and he was stormmaster and isolate.

Ferguson walked past Curran without speaking to him. He stepped off the courthouse plinth and began approaching groups in the yard, talking to them, low and earnest, some of the men looking angry, and she thought that one of them might hit him but he kept talking into their faces, his shoulders hunched as he went from group to group, gathering a shabby backstreet authority about him. Something of the bosses' hired hand about him, the strikebreaker, underhand and subtle. She saw him take one man aside and palm banknotes into his hand and after that the other man also started to approach figures in the crowd, gathering a few others to him, men starting to drift in from the afternoon shift at the shipyard in boots and caps, riveters and platemen with streaked faces and the furnace reek still about them. Patricia saw Ferguson put his hand into one man's pocket and scatter a fistful of steel rivets and bolts on the ground.

Ferguson saw Patricia.

'His nibs was on his high horse.'

'The judge?'

'The victim sitting on the edge of eternity.'

'What were you doing, talking to those men?'

'Making sure they behave themselves when the verdict comes in.'

'How do you do that?'

'I persuade them.'

'Persuade them with what? I saw you give that man money.'

'Did you? It takes more than money to keep them off the street.'

'What does it take?'

'Rain, Patricia. Rain and wind.' He looked at his watch.

'They can't find him not guilty this time, can they, Harry?'

There was movement by the courtroom doors. Reporters and spectators pushing through. A platoon of constabulary moved into position at the gates to the courthouse.

'The verdict's in,' Ferguson said. He brought Patricia around the back and they entered the courthouse through the bailiffs' postdoor. He brought her down the jury-room corridor, where a uniformed turnkey put out his hand to stop them. The whites of the man's eyes showed and his nostrils were flared.

'Pull yourself together, McMichael,' Ferguson said, 'we're only going through to the public gallery.'

'I am in dread of this day,' the man said, standing back against the wall, 'I am in mortal dread of what will be delivered from behind that door.'

Ferguson and Patricia entered the courtroom by the jury door as the public entered the gallery beside them. Curran stood at his bench in the centre of the courtroom and he saw Ferguson and his daughter enter and cross the body of the court in front of him without expression. Ferguson saw Patricia flush and he kept his own face turned away until he reached the public benches.

The courtroom filled and the tipstaff closed the doors and when he had done so the judge entered and the court rose. Once again the black silk was placed close to hand on the judge's bench and once more Taylor was led forth into the dock.

'Something's wrong. He's gone loopy,' Patricia said. Taylor nodded and smiled at his parents in the public gallery and winked at Lily's sister. The wind moaned through the tunnel from gaol to courthouse and rattled the windows and stirred dust on the scaffold planking placed so carefully against the execution-room whitewash. The jury came in with their hands down and dry leaves blew about the courtroom floor as if in parody of their dismal footfall. The foreman of the jury handed the verdict paper to the tipstaff, who brought it to the judge. The judge opened it and read it and handed it back. The foreman of the jury stood.

'In the case of Regina versus Taylor on the charge of murder, has the jury reached a verdict?'

'There is a verdict.'

'Please inform the court.'

'On the charge of murder we find the accused, Robert Taylor, guilty.'

No one in the courtroom moved. Dead leaves blew around the bench legs and the feet of the court officers. Taylor looked boyish and unconcerned. When the judge reached down for the square of black sillk Taylor rose slightly in his seat so that he could see. The judge put the silk on his head.

'Robert Taylor, I do not wish to add to the pain and anguish of the moment for you, which indeed must be great. *Dead leaves.* I shall therefore content myself with pronouncing the dread judgement and sentence of the court as prescribed by law. *It was Robert. Robert the Painter.* The sentence and judgement of the court is and it is hereby ordered and adjudged that you, Robert Taylor, be taken from the bar of the court where you now stand to his majesty's prison and that on Wednesday the sixteenth day of November in the year of our Lord one thousand nine hundred and forty-nine *babyface killer* you be taken to the common place of execution in the prison and there hanged by the neck *it's a sin to tell a lie* until you are dead and that your body be buried within the walls of the prison in which the said judgement of death shall be executed on you. And may the Lord have mercy on your soul.'

Ferguson had seen the executed at Nuremberg and had sat with the death-cell guards and their talk of hanging, the hooding, the lore of knots and drops, the crack of the trap door. He knew what he had seen. Eyeless corpses asway on crossroads gibbets at dusk. Ferguson knew that a man hearing that sentence pronounced felt the abyss open under his feet. The jury stared at Taylor with a kind of horror. Taylor looked as if he expected to be clapped from the courtroom when the jurors thought that his ears would fill with carrion acclaim, the whisper of grave tilth. Curran stood gaunt and unmoving, his eyes on Taylor. He had played his hand. He had rendered a man's soul forfeit.

No one moved. The judge wet his lips. He did not seem to know whether to remove the cap of silk or retain it.

'Bring the prisoner below,' he said. A woman screamed.

'Lily,' Patricia said. For Lily had seen what seemed to evade Taylor, the welcome of the damned, the grave's acclaim. Lily bent forward in her mourning cloth and touched her forehead to her clenched fists.

'He didn't tell her,' Ferguson said, 'Taylor didn't tell her.' He turned to Patricia.

Taylor was led out. The judge rose. Ferguson saw Curran leave the courtroom, then saw Patricia pushing her way through the public gallery.

There was a Special Constabulary cordon around the courthouse. A silent crowd stood outside it. Beyond the crowd bonfires had been lit, dull orange flame within, the smoke rolling in dark banks seaward driven by squalls inland, the smoke black as though the substance of the night were being gathered.

Patricia stopped Ferguson in the courtyard.

'You said Taylor didn't tell her. Didn't tell her what?'

'He knows he's not going to hang.'

'You did it, Harry. It's something to do with the jury. That day in Bangor. You and me. We sleuthed the jury. You took notes. Father's case. This was Father's case.'

'I was working on his behalf.'

'Were you?'

'Yes, Patricia.'

'Is it working on his behalf to cut the ground from under him?'

'Yes.'

'On whose behalf did you make me part of it? Yours or his?' He reached out to her but she moved away from him, slipping between the armed constables and into the throng. At the edge of the crowd she turned and looked back. Ferguson could see her face white against the gathering darkness, semaphore of heart's pain to come.

Ferguson found Curran at ten o'clock that evening. Curran's Lancia was parked close to the perimeter fencing at Aldergrove aerodrome. Friday night take-offs and arrivals, the smell of aviation fuel hanging in the air. Far-off lights on the apron, the red and green wingtip lights drifting off the edge of the south runway, carried into the nighttime sky, borne by the winds that blew aloft. Curran stood at the wire. A Dakota came in over his head, the undercarriage down, the turboprop exhaust blast washing over him, the fuselage alloy dented and scored, the undercarriage members chipped and oil-streaked, thundering, resolved out of the night.

Ferguson stood beside him at the wire. Curran had been in the Flying Corps at seventeen. Ferguson could see him goggled, crouched in an open cockpit. Pre-dawn briefings. Shot down over enemy lines.

'I was too young to go to France,' Curran said.

'Did you want to?'

'I lied about my age to join the Corps and they found out. My classmates all went and they all died.'

On the far side of the airfield the Dakota cut its engines and the blades whined as they slowed. A hooter sounded from the hangar area. The autumnal crosswind blew dust across the runway. Curran stood still, as if he attended to windblown anthems for the doomed of his youth.

'I won, Harry.'

'I know you won, Mr Curran. Wiped the floor with Hanna and the rest of them.'

'That's not what I mean. Every wager I made in the last three days was good. Every horse won. Every card was an ace.'

'You kept going. Making up your losses.'

'That's not it. You wait for the luck to stop. The faller at the last with the field beaten. Wagering all on a full house to turn up a two instead of an ace. That is the gamble, Ferguson. That is the full extent and material of it.'

'Hanna has filed an appeal against the guilty verdict.'

'I know.'

'It's to be heard straight away. I don't know what the grounds are.'

'Do you not know what the grounds will be, Harry? Hanna will argue that the jury were permitted an afternoon of relaxation. During that afternoon in Bangor the jury were separated one from the other. That separation is not permitted by the law. They must be kept together at all times. The lack of sequestration means that their verdict must be set aside. There is no conviction.'

'Double jeopardy means that the case cannot be tried again.'

'So Taylor is a free man.'

'Yes. Your appointment to the High Court will be announced later this week. It means that you will have no part in Taylor's appeal.'

'Attention to detail, Harry. I'm impressed. You played a bad hand well.'

'Taylor will come to some harm of his own making. His kind always do.'

'And what of our kind, Harry?'

Ferguson drove back into the city. At twelve he drove up the Malone Road. The Attorney General's car was in the driveway. All the lights were off in the house except one high up in the gable wall. Patricia's room. Ferguson drove off. Thinking about what Curran had said. Knowing that a card had been played to him and he dare not turn it over.

Twenty-two

Robert Taylor's appeal against his sentence for murder was heard on 18th December 1949 before Lord Justice Porter and Lord Justice Black. Taylor was represented by Robert Hanna QC. The new Attorney General, A. J. Reid, who had replaced Judge Lance Curran, represented the crown.

The appellants stated that jury sequestration had not been maintained during the trial. That on an outing to Bangor the members of the jury had been allowed to separate and go their separate ways and that this was forbidden by statute and in common law. Porter spoke upon the rights of the accused. He said that no blame fell upon the sergeant and constables of Leopold Street who had accompanied the members of the jury. Porter spoke about the injustice that would be done to Taylor and to his fiancée Lily if due weight was not given to the improper jury sequestration. Robert Taylor's conviction for the murder of Mary McGowan was struck out. Because he had already been tried twice for the same offence a retrial was not possible. Taylor was released.

Robert Taylor left no images of himself. When he was charged with murder he instructed his family to destroy what photographs they might have had in the house. Held on remand, he was taken from his cell in Crumlin Road to the courthouse on the other side of the road through an underground passage. On his few public appearances a coat or a solicitor's file concealed his features. Taylor knew the odds.

Twenty-three

MARCH 1961

Esther met Capstick from the Heathrow flight at Aldergrove. There were snow flurries as the plane touched down on the runway. The light snow formed vortices in the rotor wash. Esther waited for him on the apron, the Viscount taxiing to a halt, the passengers disembarking into the frozen night. They did not speak until they were driving back into the city.

'What's your game, Mrs Ferguson?'

'I want to know the truth about Patricia.'

'There's more to it.'

'Why do you say that?'

'Because there always is.'

'Curran's about to try a capital murder case. A man called McGladdery, for the murder of a nineteen-year-old shop girl.'

'The same age as Patricia.'

'McGladdery doesn't have a hope with Curran on the bench.'

'You think it's not just.'

'Curran will hang him.'

'Is this McGladdery something to you?'

'No.'

'Then why all this? You trying to get back at Harry? He's still Curran's man, isn't he?'

Capstick turned his head to smile at Esther, his face lit by oncoming headlights, fleshy, corrupted. Examining her in the unforgiving light. The corners of her mouth lined. Her eyes in darkness.

'He's still Curran's man.'

'For Patricia then?'

'I don't have to explain myself to you, do I?'

'You done all the explaining you needed to do a long time ago.' Esther seeing the hotel bedroom. Captstick lying on the bed. Esther sitting at the dressing table in her slip. Her face in the mirror. The ineradicable shadow.

'I called you for Harry. I want the harm to stop. I don't want Lance Curran hanging a man and my husband going along with it.'

'You can drop me at the hotel,' Capstick said. 'I'll find my own way out to Holywell.'

'Will she tell you?'

'They generally do. Does Ferguson know you called me?'

'No.'

'Are you going to keep it that way?' She didn't answer. She left him at the International Hotel. Ferguson was waiting for her in the living room. Her medical file from Holywell lay on the card table. She opened it and read in silence.

'Where is Capstick?' He said.

'At his hotel. How did you know?' Ferguson shrugged. The furtive ways of the city his stock in trade.

'What else do you know? Do you know who killed Patricia?'

'No.'

Esther said that she had had an abortion when she was eighteen. Backstreet stuff. He knew about it from Germany. The hunched-over agonies. The scraping and scouring, the risk of things pierced, things rupturing, the haemorrhagic flow. A midwife, a matronly figure carrying a leather bag, leaving the house after dark, closing the door carefully.

It wasn't that, she said, it was a clinic. In a good street in London. Everyone was very discreet. But they messed it up anyway.

'When I got back home they said I was a nymphomaniac. They sent me to the asylum. To the actual loony bin.'

She was released a month before she met Ferguson. She had slept with him in seaside hotels, travelling up the coast where they would not be recognised, taking the illicit into their relationship. She would drink whiskey and soda. In bed she would speak obscenities into his ear, describe sex acts he had never heard of. During the day she was silent and withdrawn. She took his hand in restaurants and put it between her legs.

'Holywell.'

'Yes.'

Ferguson held her hand until she fell asleep. Their marriage had been an accord on her hurt. They would tend it together. He put a blanket over her and left her and went outside to his car. He looked towards the dark of the mountains beyond the city. There was a line of stars along the sharp cut edge of the Black Mountain as though darkness struck fire in the deep basalt.

*

Doris was surprised to learn that she had a visitor on Wednesday evening. There were seldom visitors during the week and there were never visitors after five. The night was hers alone. The duty nurse took her from her room to the day room. She was unaccustomed to being there at nighttime and found it cold and ill-lit. She did not recognise the man at first and he smiled at her in a most unpleasant way. Mr Brown came in with him but the man told him to go.

'Capstick of the Yard is known for solo results, Mr Brown,' he said. 'Your presence is not required.'

Chief Inspector Capstick.

Doris recalled it had been Capstick who took the confession from Iain Hay Gordon when he was accused of murdering Patricia. Not that a frail man such as Gordon could have done murder against Patricia with her waspish temperament. She had never met Capstick but had always thought of him as a vulgar man acquainted with many of the lowest types.

'Good to see you looking so well, Doris. I heard you were a bit shook, but the rest has done you good.'

'My needs have been well attended to, Chief Inspector.'

'You'd be well used to a place like this, Doris, wouldn't you? I'd say you seen plenty when you lived in Broadmoor. Plenty of lunatic behaviour.'

'I had a sheltered upbringing, Mr Capstick.'

'What I'm trying to get at is this. It wouldn't be too hard for you to put on. It wouldn't be out of the picture for you to act like you'd lost your marbles when you were as sane as the next man or woman.'

'I don't understand you, Chief Inspector.'

'Don't give me that, Doris. You understand me plain as day. Many's the place like this I sat in listening to some miscreant trying to get his neck out of a noose. You know damn well what happened to Patricia.'

'I am not one of your creatures, Chief Inspector, one of your criminals from the slums and suburbs. I am Doris Curran and I will be Lady Curran.'

'Hark at her, brought up in the loony bin.'

'I must object.'

'You can object all you like, Doris, there's nobody listening. I know all about you and your daughter. She was a saucy little article and no mistake, isn't that right?'

'You have no right to speak to me like that.'

'I'll speak to you any way I choose. I met many a little madam like your Patricia when I was working the West End. A posh little minx on the skinny for some rough trade. Thought they was different from the rest of us but they all look more or less the same when they're on their back, if you get my drift.'

'You are a horrid man.'

'Horrid I may well be, but I don't see you breaking down. There's no waterworks for our Patricia. That's missing from this here scene. Any mother would be in bits at this stage but not our Doris.'

'Stop it.'

'I didn't leave my daughter lying dead on the leafy forest floor. I didn't pretend she was still alive when she was as stiff as a plank. So what's the story here, Doris? Which one of you done her in? Or maybe all of you done it.'

'I did not harm my daughter. I did not. I did not.'

'So you say, but old Judge Curran, he must of reckoned you done her in, the way he acted.'

'Nurse, nurse, nurse.'

'Don't get me wrong, Doris. Far as I can see Patricia was a goner, no matter what. Some girls just have that. You know they're going to end up in an alley with their skirt over their head. It's in their nature to be tarts. They smell danger and danger smells them and there's nothing no one can do about it. What gets me is that you rotten lot would have let the hangman have Gordon before you'd rat each other out.'

Capstick stood up and took a black notebook from his open pocket. 'These is from your police files, Thomas Cutbush. Also known as Jack the Ripper. Also known as Saucy Jack. *When officers from Scotland Yard entered Cutbush's lodgings at the Minories they conducted a thorough search. In the chimney piece they apprehended pieces of woman's attire stained with blood. Three cami skirts. Two overskirts. Other ladies' sundries equally stained with blood.*'

'Vile, Chief Inspector. Utterly vile.'

'*Officers also seized an amount of anatomy books with the pages being soiled at illustrations of the intimate female parts. Among the items taken from the chimney breast were two anatomical drawings of women, one of them displaying mutilations.*'

'You will stop this, Chief Inspector. My husband is an important man. He will hear of this.'

'You're the tricky one and no mistake, Doris. There was more than one minx in the Curran family if you want my opinion.'

In the suspect's possession at the time of his arrest was a 'Polish knife', very sharp with a bone handle.

'I'll do you, Cutbush.'

When suspect was removed to Broadmoor Hospital for the criminally insane he informed staff and inmates that he would 'rip them all'.

She was locked up *like Cutbush.* She was a watcher from windows *like Cutbush.* She knew what Saucy Jack would do to the

Chief Inspector. Jack would have the knives out. Chop chop. What odds would be given for your life then, Chief Inspector? You'd be rent from your ball sack to your gizzard. Chop chop. When Thomas Cutbush asks for silence he gets silence.

Doris looked up. There was someone else in the room. Another watcher. How long had he been there? Ferguson. Lance's man. He of the slut wife. The man she had seen from her window as he left Patricia home late at night. The man she had seen searching the forest on the night Patricia died.

'I think that's enough, Chief Inspector.' Capstick turned.

'That's a crying shame, Ferguson. I had her on the ropes there. Another few minutes I would have had her telling me every last thing. They want to, you know. Her ladyship might hide all she likes but she's as bent as a nine-bob note.'

'Your flight's booked for eight o'clock in the morning.'

'Fair enough, Ferguson. It's your funeral. Mind you, if old Doris ever gets out I'd keep that wife of yours locked up. Not to be trusted, our Doris.'

Twenty-four

'Lucy took the flowers back.'

'What did you say, Mrs Curran?' Doris had fallen asleep in a wingback chair. Ferguson sitting in the window seat beside her.

'She was afraid that Father would ask where they came from and she would get into trouble for not looking after me.'

'Lucy?'

'The housemaid. She looked after me when Mother wasn't well.'

'What flowers were they?'

'Pink roses. In the middle of winter.'

'Where did you get pink roses in winter?'

'I asked him for them. He brought me into the shed.'

'Who did you ask for them?'

'Jack.'

'Who was he? One of the gardeners?'

'Lucy took the flowers back to Jack. I think he was waiting for her.'

'Who was Jack, Mrs Curran?'

'Lucy never came back to me, Mr Ferguson.'

'You never saw her again?'

'There was a different maid the next day. She wasn't like Lucy. She never chatted to me or let me put on lipstick when Father wasn't there.'

'Did anyone tell you what happened to her?'

'No.' Although Doris could guess what happened to Lucy in the shed. Among the rakes and spades and packets of seed spilled, the bulbs and corms. In the darkness.

Doris had closed her eyes again. Her breathing was even. Her chest rose and fell. Even so, Ferguson did not think that she was asleep.

That's a cheeky lie, Doris Curran, Lucy said. *You did see me again.*

Doris didn't know what Lucy had done to end up in Broadmoor, what sad tale she was part of, an infanticide perhaps, a baby unwanted plunged in water or left to die in bitter cold. Lucy moved without noise around the house and told her tales of murder dark and desperate but always Cutbush, she always came back to him.

Lucy said Thomas Cutbush killed six women and cut them all to shreds, he took their innards out their womanly parts and took them home for to play with. What did they call him? Doris had asked. Saucy Jack, Lucy replied, and he were right saucy too.

At full moon all the patients were put on lockdown, Lucy said, but Doris knew that. Father said that there was a draw on the fluids of the brain at the apex of the lunar cycle. You could stand outside on a full moon night and hear them moan and cry out. Father said that some paced their cell all night. Or sat on their bunks rocking. But not Cutbush. Nothing stirred in his cell.

Doris knows what they think in Holywell, that butter wouldn't melt in her mouth. They all forget where she was brought up. Broadmoor prison for the criminally insane. That's no picnic, Lucy says.

Father showed her everything. The table with the leather straps where you were tied down for ECT. The copper skullcap and the piece of black rubber to put in your mouth so that you wouldn't bite your tongue when they gave you the full twenty-five thousand volts. No messing around there, Lucy said.

'Lance would have made a good Jack the Ripper, wouldn't he, Mr Ferguson?'

'What do you mean?' But Ferguson knew what she meant. He could see Lance at large in the Whitechapel night, a shadow in himself, bound to harm. Women beckoning from doorways. What stakes would they play for? Jack dicing with them in the darkness. The soul-wagers. Lance would stake what the darkness demanded and he would pay his forfeit.

'Tell me about Cutbush, Mrs Curran,' Ferguson said.

'I told you to be quiet. You don't want to meet him. You don't want to meet Saucy Jack.'

'Saucy Jack?'

'That's what he called himself when it happened to Doris.'

'What happened to her?'

'Doris went into the shed and didn't come out.'

'She got the roses.'

'Yes.'

'But Lucy took them back.'

'Yes.'

'And you never saw Lucy again.'

Now, now, Doris Curran. Tell the truth and shame the devil.

'There was a woman. Against the wire. She had no clothes on.'

'It was Lucy?'

'After she came back from the shed.' It was freezing that night. The ground was frosted. Lucy stood barefoot and naked in the exercise yard. Two warders approached her. One of them took off his overcoat and put it over her shoulders.

'What did Jack do to Lucy in the shed, Mrs Curran?'

'He sported with her. The way he sported with the lasses under the arches at Whitechapel.'

'What did he do to Doris?'

Not answered.

'Did Patricia ring you from the bus stop on the night she died?'

Not answered.

'Did you take the car down to pick her up?'

Not answered.

Doris played families every day when she was small. That was what Patricia did not understand. There was a father. Sometimes there was a son. But there was always a mother and a daughter. Standing a little apart from the others, looking at each other, speaking a secret mother and daughter language. When she was seventeen she bought a clutch purse in the Army and Navy stores and could see a daughter carrying it. It was about making store against the future. She bought stockings still in their wrappers. Other girls had their trousseaus, their glory boxes where they kept household items, linens, tableware. But Doris wanted more than that. She had a picture in her head of a daughter, a companion. They would shop together. They would take tea, be disdainful of the other ladies, have a secret language of nods and gestures that only they understood. Doris would produce the items she had bought and they would be unwrapped with noises of delight.

'Who killed Patricia, Mrs Curran?' Ferguson leaned close to her.

'I know,' Doris said, 'I know who did it.'

'Tell me. I won't repeat it.'

'I know you won't repeat it. To tell you is to tell the darkness.'

'Who did it, Doris?' Ferguson was aware of the night around them. That they sat alone in the empty recreation room. Around them the table-tennis tables, the stacked board games. That the shadows made sport there.

'Cutbush.' Doris whispered the name. 'Cutbush did it.'

*

Esther woke when Ferguson came home. She sat up and gathered the blanket around her, brushed her hair back from her forehead. Every time he came home late was the same as the night he came in to tell her that Patricia had been murdered. The same pain in his face.

'Did she kill Patricia?'

'By her own words. She says Cutbush, but she is Cutbush in her own head.'

'Poor Doris.'

'Poor Patricia.'

'What happened to Taylor?'

'They say he went to Canada with Lily but I don't believe it.'

Taylor and his box of tricks. *If harm had a human face.* Out there somewhere with his pinchings and rubbings. Staying clear of the dog tracks. Now he knew what such dogs were for. Now he knew what it was like to be hunted, the yelps and snuffles, the unrelenting padding on your trail, on your scent. Taylor knew better than to let his face be seen in public. Men like Lunn and McKenzie wouldn't have it. Men like Hanna.

Ferguson had heard that Taylor had moved to the eastern periphery of the city, into one of the new housing estates built for the growing population of the city. The privet gardens and new shopfronts in need of their own hauntings. Taylor a figure of storybook malice. Lily the veiled lady.

'I wish they'd hanged him.'

'Do you?'

'If they had Lance Curran wouldn't have been a judge.'

'And Patricia might still be alive.'

'Sometimes I wonder if she ever existed. If I dreamed her.'

'She existed. There's a stone in the graveyard to say it.'

'Can we stop Curran trying McGladdery?'

'No. Doris told me that Cutbush did it. She didn't tell Capstick. Doris might be sick but she's not stupid.'

'Loyal to Curran.'

'More loyal than me, you mean.'

'She is his wife, Harry.'

1ST OCTOBER 1963

Basilica of St John, Rome

The ordinands kneel in a semicircle before the altar. The bishop is seated on his faldstool before them, the folds of his surplice spread on the ground.

Receive the yoke of the Lord for His yoke is sweet and His burden light.

Lancelot Curran is seated to the left of the altar. His son Desmond is among the kneeling supplicants. Befrocked priests move in the annexed chapels. Lance Curran sits without moving. The rite must be endured. The litany moves on. The candidates prostrate themselves, their faces pressed to the marble floor. The dominion of centuries presses down on them. Idolatrous chants in the septs of Rome.

There is instruction here. On the decline of empires. His son receives benedictions. The priests move in procession. They stretch out their hands to take the oils. They say they have shriven themselves of sin and are dressed in white. Curran knows that sin is never erased.

Curran has made his play and now he gathers his winnings to him. His son a Romish priest. His wife a madwoman. His daughter murdered.

On 16th October 1961 Judge Lance Curran had sentenced Robert McGladdery to death for the murder of Pearl Gamble.

Curran's summing up left no doubt in the jury's mind that McGladdery had murdered Pearl Gamble. They returned with a guilty verdict after forty minutes' deliberation. Robert McGladdery was hanged in Crumlin Road prison on 20th December 1961.

The novices kneel on the floor then fall forward on to their faces, their arms outspread. Curran watches his son's submission. In hours to come his son will bless him, his hands made fragrant with oils of chrism, with oils of myrrh. Desmond's soutane is spread out. In a side chapel the garments of authority are made ready for him.

2ND OCTOBER 1963

The phone rang. Calls in the night. Time after time the summons comes at night. Ferguson thinks that the last call to judgement will be such a summons. That Patricia might hearken to it and be raised. Even the eyeless succubus in her painted chest would pay heed. He had heard the voice at the other end of the line twenty-four years hence and it had not changed and he felt the malice in it. Why now? He remembered the photograph in the Telegraph that day. The Judge and his priest son.

Ferguson expected and was given a time and a place. He went to his car. The dread rendezvous. He drove along the lough shore in the dark. The masthead lights of ships showed beyond the bar. He could see night waves on the shoal rocks, their surge and billow. He stopped at the gates of the Glen. He crossed the road to the telephone box, its frail light votive in the gathered dark. As the caller had said there was a manilla envelope on the directory shelf. He opened the envelope and slid from it a charcoal drawing of a nude woman. A life drawing. The woman sat with her legs under her, head turned away, haunch and breast exposed. The phone rang. The same voice as before. Taylor. *The button man.*

'You found the envelope, Mr Ferguson?'

'Where did you get this drawing, Taylor?'

'I seen her sitting beside you at the trial. Reckon she was more than just the boss's daughter.'

'Where did you get it?'

'The night she got killed she was carrying a folder. Books.

A yellow cap.'

'A Juliet cap.'

'That's it. They weren't there, were they, when the body was found?'

'The drawing, Taylor.'

'Curran made a cod out of me in the witness box. I told him what I knew but he wouldn't stop.'

'You never went to Canada. You waited for Patricia on the driveway.'

'I seen Curran at the bookies and the dog track. Acting like he was better than all of us when he was the same or worse.'

'You pulled her into the trees.'

'Curran hanged that boy McGladdery. She would have sat there and watched her da put on the black cap the way he had the judge put it on for me.'

'Patricia.'

'Stuck up. Who did she think she was? I seen the way she looked at me. Like I was dirt. There's only one answer to that.'

'Did you take the drawing from her folder?'

'They're all the same when they're on their back and they're all the same when they're lying in heart's blood. I kept that drawing in the box of tricks special for you, Mr Ferguson. I knew you'd like a souvenir of the dear departed. Mightn't be the first souvenir you got off her.'

Taylor was still talking when Ferguson put the phone down. He had never considered Taylor as a suspect in Patricia's murder. He had never thought that Taylor or another man unknown to him, some enemy of Curran, had hidden in the trees to wait for Patricia. Now it seemed as likely as any other conclusion. Taylor. Doris. Cutbush. Lancelot Curran. They had gathered about

Patricia. They had made a fellowship of themselves. He thought that if one of them had not taken her life, then another would have stepped forward. He opened the telephone-box door on to the pavement. To his left the driveway led through the woods where Patricia had been found to the house now shuttered and unseen. The Glen. The Judge's house.

The phone would ring again. His life had been made of such appointments. Men who bade him come to them that they might show how they had mastered the world when the truth was that they always had attended on his will. The rich and the beggared. The guilty and innocent. Those who had been bought. Those who had been sold.

He looked down at the drawing. The nude woman crouched, alert. Ready for flight.

Some days after Taylor had been released Ferguson had seen Patricia on University Road with a group of schoolfriends. In their uniforms of pleated skirts and seamed stockings they seemed aloof and knowing. In the evenings when they had gone home to Malone and Holywood, the silken boroughs, they left a little of themselves behind to the night settling in on the university streets, the ghosts of longing abroad in the dark. Years after Patricia's death Ferguson would walk these streets and think that she was there somewhere, close by in the dusk. Patricia had not waited at the courthouse on the day of Taylor's conviction. Nor had he ever been alone in her company again. After her murder stories had reached him of Patricia's men. Of her reputed promiscuity. These men had never shown themselves and he had never found them. But they would be forever her companions in the dark. In this faithless city the story was all.

Acknowledgement

The author would like to acknowledge his debt to Tom McAlindon's *Bloodstains in Ulster*, the authoritative account of the Robert Taylor affair.

Also in Eoin McNamee's 'Blue' Trilogy

The Blue Tango

At 2.20am on the morning of the 13th November 1952 the body of nineteen-year-old Patricia Curran was carried into the surgery belonging to the family doctor. At first Dr Kenneth Wilson thought that she'd been the victim of an accidental shooting. In fact a subsequent post-mortem revealed that she had been stabbed thrity-seven times.

The Blue Tango is at once a gripping thriller and a *danse macabre* through a shadowy world of corruption and sexual intrigue – a darkly lyrical narrative of white mischief in post-war Ireland, of false accusation and savage murder, presided over by the haunted, tragic figure of Patricia Curran.

LONGLISTED FOR THE BOOKER PRIZE

'The finest novel published by any Irish writer this year and for many years.' Eileen Battersby, *Irish Times*

'This is a beautifully written book . . . you will not put it down.' *Irish Independent*

'Such verbal polish adds to the thrill of the crime story, giving it the black and wicked glitter of jet.' *Sunday Times*

ff

Orchid Blue

A haunting novel, exploring a notorious true-life murder case which resulted in the last hanging in Northern Ireland.

January 1961. The beaten, stabbed and strangled body of nineteen-year-old Pearl Gamble is discovered after a dance the previous night at Newry Orange Hall. The town is eager for justice, and local man Robert McGladdery is soon arrested.

But Detective Eddie McCrink, freshly returned from London, begins to suspect that the investigation is being influenced from the outside. And when Lord Justice Curran – whose own nineteen-year-old daugher was murdered nine years earlier in strangely similar circumstances – is assigned to try the case, it becomes increasingly difficult for everyone involved to separate the tragedies of the past from the crimes of the present.

'Heartstopping, brilliant. McNamee works the line between crime and literature.' Christopher Fowler, *Financial Times* Books of the Year

'Hypnotic . . . A sinister, shocking shadowplay.' Val McDermid

'What begins as a crime thriller gradually builds into a political novel of the highest order.' John Burnside, *Guardian*